Initiation

Published in Canada by Fitzhenry & Whiteside, 195 Allstate Parkway,
Markham, Ontario L3R 4T8

Published in the United States by Fitzhenry & Whiteside,
121 Harvard Avenue, Suite 2, Allston, Massachusetts 02134

www.fitzhenry.ca   godwit@fitzhenry.ca

National Library of Canada Cataloguing in Publication

Schwartz, Virginia Frances
Initiation / Virginia Frances Schwartz ; cover illustration, Paul Morin.

ISBN 1-55005-053-2 (bound)—ISBN 1-55005-054-0 (pbk.)

1. Kwakiutl children—Juvenile fiction. 2. Kwakiutl Indians—Juvenile
fiction. I. Morin, Paul, 1959- II. Title.

PS8587.C5786I54 2003   jC813'.6   C2003-901935-7
PZ7

U.S. Cataloging-in-Publication Data
(Library of Congress Standards)

Schwartz, Virginia Frances.
Initiation / Virginia Frances Schwartz.—1st ed.
[278] p. : cm.
Summary: On the brink of adulthood, Nana and her twin brother face a certain
future. Daughter of a proud Kwakiutl chief, she will be sold in marriage to another
tribe while her twin brother Nanolatch stays behind to become a warrior chief.
ISBN 1-55005-053-2
ISBN 1-55005-054-0   (pbk.)
1. Kwakiutl Indians — Fiction. 2. Coming of age — Fiction. 3. Twins — Fiction.
I. Title.
[Fic] 21   PZ7.S4114In 2003

Fitzhenry & Whiteside acknowledges with thanks the Canada Council for the Arts,
the Government of Canada through the Book Publishing Industry Development
Program (BPIDP), and the Ontario Arts Council for their support for
our publishing program.

Design by Wycliffe Smith Design Inc.
Cover illustration by Paul Morin
Printed in Canada

Initiation

BY Virginia Frances Schwartz

Fitzhenry & Whiteside

For Julie who is becoming
&
for Ganesha
Remover of Obstacles

V.F.S.

The New World, Northwest Coast

Blessing of the Twins

1440, SALISH VILLAGE

NOH

Ravens flew above my head. Countless. Like black thunder, their caws crackled in my ears. Again and again they pounded, throwing me to the sand. I covered my ears. But still they cried. Then the darkness dropped down, and out of it, the brother and sister appeared.

Mother says not to be afraid, for I have had a vision. I have seen something far off and long ago. It happened when they cut my face and threaded needles into my bare flesh. They pushed a trail of charcoal powder beneath my skin. Tattoos to forever mark me.

But I know not what this vision is or why it came, only that I saw the two of them....

*

The girl did not know that on the day she was born all those years ago, her brother leaped into the world an hour before her. He spun—dazzling in the air, slippery wet, his body reddened from his journey—before he landed with a flop in his mother's arms.

Firstborn. Son of the chief.

The tribe rejoiced with the birth of this boy, heir to wealth. But an old wrinkled woman, a grandmother perhaps, coaxed the mother to lie still. She set her ear on the younger woman's swollen belly. She listened to sounds no one in the birthing house noticed in the midst of all the rejoicing. She heard a loud splashing of water, like someone swimming to shore from far out at sea. In the next hour another child was born with long legs and a great cry.

Secondborn. Daughter of the chief's wife. The grandmother smiled and lifted the baby to her chest. The tribe cheered.

The brother and sister did not know there was a ceremony when their mother left the village with twin babies in her arms. All the nearby clans on the northwest coast journeyed upriver to the fishing grounds to see them. It was special magic to look upon Salmon Twins there.

This girl will be given the gift of a memory. That will be the beginning of her remembering.

She will remember being carried with her brother through fir woods in a shining place. Beneath her, the river roared. Chinook salmon teemed in the water, beating their fins with the rhythm of drumbeats. They leaped over the waterfall one by one. Spears glinted in the sunlight. Warriors lifted the twins up higher and higher to touch the sun. The girl landed with a flop in her father's arms.

She will remember more.

*

This is what I know of them and nothing more.

They will be older now, but the two share the same face. Whenever they look at one another, they will sense the place they came from. Skin darkened like polished bark from living by the sea. Earth brown eyes. Straight white teeth. Cheekbones high and carved like cliff stone. Long black hair trailing down both their backs like a thick snake, flying in the wind like something wild.

They will enter a time of passage in their lives, the journey from childhood to adulthood. Their initiation.

It is a time of transit. Of secrecy. Of migration. Their lives are the thread between reality and magic.

Tightly woven like a spider's web.

Thick enough to trap the truth.

Thin enough for a story to blow through.

Place of Mists

CHAPTER 1

Breaking of the Way

1441, KWAKIUTL VILLAGE

NANA

Shilka says there are warriors who eat up the evil of the world, wipe our memories away, so we can start again.

Atone.

I wish that warrior would find his way into our winter village now. Creep along the secret paths from the mountains down to our shoreline and free us. Slice through this endless fog like a sharp knife. Step along the sand where the silent totem poles watch.

Break the spell.

For beyond our village, the seas are stirred up.

I wish I had not been at the tribal gathering last

night in the Winter Ceremonial House. All the
Raven Clan was seated in front of the fire in endless
circles of Kwakiutls, fanning out like wings. Each by
rank. Shilka, our shaman, in front. Taises, my royal
family, nearest the fire. My father, the chief, his face
aflame, flanked by my mother, graceful in her Chinook salmon robes. Between Grandmother and my
brother, I sank into my spot.

My brother and I have been one unbroken shadow running ahead of the sun these eleven years
since our twin birth. When someone called me, he
looked up too. My brother Nanolatch is "He Who
Leaps with the Salmon." Nana means "Salmonwife"
but no one ever calls me that. It is my sacred name.
When you say it aloud, you set the spirits loose.

You can never predict what will happen then.

First Uncle, usually smiling, was grim faced that
night. In the firelight, his bare chest gleamed with
fish etchings. Each one a story painted on. Tales of
sockeye and spring Chinook caught. My brother
knew them all by heart and never tired of hearing
them. He believed that First Uncle could do anything, even be that warrior who will save our tribe.
Nanolatch would become his shadow, leaving my
side, if First Uncle allowed it.

Second Uncle was a silent man who always sat
apart. He motioned to my squirming cousins next to
us to be quiet. The Lequiltok, a Kwakiutl tribe from
the south, were seated opposite us, dressed in long,
cedar traveling capes. Warriors guarded us. The

michimis, commoners like the fishwives and fishermen, sat in darkness at our backs. By the door,
blocking the wind and damp, crouched the slaves.

I thought we would have a potlatch, rejoicing.
Passing mussel shells steamed in kelp broth. Swal-
lowing seal meat sweetened with dried salmonberries. Eating and singing, dancing all night. Instead,
we were seated straight-backed, listening.

"The Salish have fouled the sea. Done what
should not be done!"

When my father speaks, it is thunder. He stood
halfway up to the pointed roof of the Ceremonial
House. Everyone looked up at his dark face. Everyone shifted back to give him space.

"Those Salish are everywhere. Far inland do
they reach," Second Uncle told us. "But these were
Coast Salish who canoed from just below Kwakiutl
territory, a six-day journey."

"What have the lazy ones done?" Shilka
demanded. The shaman banged his staff down, stabbing the sand.

It was not easy to look at his horrible face,
thickly painted, or even to guess his age. Not one of
the elders remembers when he was born. He looked
like neither man nor woman and was so crooked
that he leaned on a staff wherever he went.

"We have seen these Salish out at sea, luring
salmon from their house," Father told him. "Their
canoes were loaded with the Sacred Ones that travel
up the rivers to the mountains to bear us salmon."

Oh, I thought, they have reached down into the Country Beyond the Ocean. Forbidden! Out where the Salmon Men grow. No one can fish there. From spring to fall, salmon will journey to lay a thousand eggs upriver.

"How many were seen?" Shilka demanded.

"Five canoes brimful," said First Uncle. "The light-skinned ones paddled fiercely away when they saw us. They headed south, the wind behind them."

"This cannot be. The Way says to take enough food, no more," protested the Lequiltok chief. "One halibut hooked can be so heavy, it feeds our whole tribe for a week."

Second Uncle's chest rose up full, like he was in battle. "That is not the worst of it! We spied on their village many days later, past Lequiltok land. Behind their cedar homes they had dropped piles of fish skeletons with the sun shining full upon them."

My brother's mouth fell open. He stared back and forth at each of our uncles, not wanting to believe this was true. Taboo.

Shilka's thin lips stretched back as if in pain. "Never to be done! All bones must be returned to the waters from where they came. The Way is broken!"

The Way. For every act, there follows another like a dog at our heels. Spit upon the Spirits in Heaven and it will fall back down upon your head as rain. This is the law that works like day following night, sunrise falling down to sunset. No way to stop it once it begins. Obey the Way and we will be rewarded. The salmon will run strong. The winters will be mild, the summers long. Disobey and all balance is gone.

"These Salish must pay!" First Uncle called out. "We will force them to give us their catch so we will have enough to eat if the salmon fail."

Shilka screeched, his toothless mouth as pointed as a hawk's beak. "Their catch is fouled. Eat one bite of it and the Ekas will rip your soul apart!"

The taises squirmed in their places. At the mention of the evil spirits' name, we all flinched. Even the murmuring of the fishwives was silenced.

"Kill them!" a Lequiltok warrior screamed.

One by one, I heard the cries of men echo around the fire-pit.

"Burn their village!"

"Capture them!"

Then I heard her voice. It reminded me of the wind turning on a cool spring afternoon. How it blows from the south, touching your skin, warm and soft, smelling of rain.

"If you kill another, someone will avenge their death." Grandmother rose up. "There will be no end to the killing."

She is the only woman allowed to speak at tribal council. She is the chief's mother, ancient one, dressed in a plain cedar cape, her only ornament a bone nose ring. Perhaps she once was tall but now she is worn down like a shell on the beach. A million lines mark her face, of wind and sun and sea air.

They call her Flies on Wind. When she was young, she had a vision of her spirit soaring up to the spirits. Some say she walks there still, her feet up in the air.

"This is what our ancestors taught, those who ride high on the wind with the ravens. Does anyone hear them?" she questioned. "Great-grandfather gave us a sign: when the twins near their Initiation, he predicted, we will witness great changes. Do not act. Do not kill."

My brother nudged me. Grandmother was speaking about our Initiation, when we would become adults of the Raven Clan. It had seemed so distant until that moment.

"The ancestors lived in a different time," said Second Uncle. "The salmon have been taken from us. We must avenge them and go to war."

"Our ancestors killed and warred too," Grandmother argued. "My father died at Bella Coola hands. My brothers were killed by the Haida. It is their voices I hear now. Killing did not bring them back. Wait, they say."

Shilka stepped up to Grandmother. He hissed like a cougar, spit flying in the air.

"We need to act! What do you say we should do?"

A voice inside me answered but no one heard.

Do not kill the innocents.

"Listen to the spirits," advised Grandmother. "They will show us what to do. If you must root out evil, punish only the ones you saw that day at sea.

Sacrifice them, not all their people."

"What say you, Shilka?" First Uncle demanded.

"The Salish in that coastal village must all die."

"What say you, warriors?" Second Uncle called out.

One by one, our tribe, and then the Lequiltok, lifted their spears and pounded them down on the sand bottom of the house.

"Kill! Kill! Kill all of them!"

My whole body shook. I wanted to reach for my mother, crouched in my father's cold shadow. Whatever he decided, we must all obey.

My father's voice boomed like a beating war drum. "We go to war by the next full moon. Lequiltok, return to your village and ready your warriors for the journey. We put to sea with all our men."

The fishermen shouted and raised their arms, fists clenched. The Ceremonial House swayed, creaking on its cedar poles. Grandmother sank down to the sand. It drew tears from my soul just to look at her.

Something sharp twisted in my chest, piercing me through and through.

We will go to war. No warrior will swallow this evil like magic. No one will listen to the spirits anymore.

There will be no end to the blood.

CHAPTER 2

Lightning Raid

NANOLATCH

Three long war canoes line the shore. They are
loaded with yew clubs, spears, water sacks, and
dried fish for the journey. All day long I carted these
supplies with the michimis and slaves across the
beach for First Uncle, until my legs quivered like
bowstrings. We worked fast. On winter days there
are just a few hours of light. Our village hides
beneath clouds. The warriors shouted orders in the
rain; and in the plankhouses, already the women
began to mourn.

Tonight the full moon will rise and they will be
gone.

I stop at dusk and think how I could just keep

running like this, my heart beating wildly like a marmot caught in a snare. Snap like a lightning rod to the spot where First Uncle points. Fly bare-chested, heated with my work even in this chill wind. Hand him a tool before he says a word.

I tell no one about our midnight ride. Late last night, just the two of us sneaked to the beach while our families slept. We passed by the tideline where heavy ocean canoes and many long river canoes were pulled up. With one hand First Uncle lifted a two-man canoe, narrow as an eel, and set it to sea. Soon we dipped our paddles down into darkness. We passed the bay where the whitecaps rolled, rocking us from side to side. Even the wind fought us, smacking our faces. But I did not mind. The stars were so low and close that I could open my mouth and swallow them whole.

First Uncle pointed to the darkened Salmon House, a far distance off.

"The light will return," he promised me. "Though the sea is fouled, the salmon will run strong again. Always they came to us, one after another. Chinook. Sockeye. Pink. Dog. Coho. They will run again some day upriver."

He sighed as if he was tired. I knew I could ask him anything—unlike Father or Second Uncle, who would ignore me.

"What can I do to help?"

He turned then, looking through me like a totem

pole that stares endless deep.

"Run and fish. Make your body strong."

I leaned closer, not breathing. I waited, wanting to be just like him.

"You will become the greatest fisherman this tribe has known," he said.

"But," I begged him, "won't I be a warrior like you some day?"

He shivered and looked away. "If the spirits swallow evil in this battle, you will be safe. Pray it is so."

We have not spoken since. His words branding me, hushing the million questions I would have asked.

Now the moon lifts up, round and bright, for all to see our fiercest warrior, Second Uncle. His face is blackened, thick with charcoal. Only the whites of his eyes shine. His long hair is gathered into a knot high on top his head. A hemlock stick is jabbed through it.

Father swirls to call his warriors. Then he studies me, reading me like he does the weather at sea. His face is leaner than usual, circles darkening beneath his eyes. All week he has been too stirred up to even glance my way. He has been the churned-up waters of a storm, heaving everything and everyone out of his way.

Until this moment. The canoes are brimful with weapons. Thirty warriors, clothed in cedar-rimmed hats and cloaks to fight the mists, the women rising out of the plankhouses as if roused from sleep.

My father, his face red-streaked with war lines, sets his hands on my shoulders. My whole body lifts up to his touch. His bark brown eyes soften for the first time.

"My son. You are growing strong. You will be a great warrior someday."

"Take me with you," I beg him. "Let me ride by your side this time."

Father's chest rises full and then falls flat.

"Next time I go on a raid, you will come. First, you must train. Ready yourself for manhood with First Uncle upon our return."

First Uncle, his cheeks streaked thick with red ochre, nods. "You will begin your Initiation soon and live in my house. I will teach you what you long to know."

I won't tell him I saw him run out of the woods at dawn. His flesh raw and red from dipping into the icy stream, so freezing it cuts your breath. Afterward, he headed to the fire-pit in the Ceremonial House. I leaned into the doorway to watch. He beat upon his bare skin with hemlock branches until it drew blood. Such is what he will ask me to do one day.

The breath leaks out of me, my jaws tense from tightening so long. I look up to the many inches I must grow to meet First Uncle's eye. To hold such a harpoon as his, its bone tip gleaming white in the moonlight. I see the trials ahead of me and vow—I will pass them.

Next time I will go, Father promised. I must ready myself.

The women surround us now, pale-faced and solemn. Black ash lines mark their foreheads and cheeks. My mother's eyes brighten in the mist. She must live quietly while the war party is gone to keep them in the spirits' favor. Success in war depends upon the women at home.

Shilka raises his staff and chants in the ancient language. He flings spells, words that croak in the damp air. All the warriors bow their heads.

"Avenge!" he tells them. "Return safe, each one of you."

The water drifts away from our feet. The wind picks up. Warriors step into canoes and the fishermen push them off. I shove my father's canoe, shoulder to shoulder with the men. The canoes fly. Straight south to meet the Lequiltok. Then farther south to Salish lands.

We all stand like totem poles silently looking out to sea. Wives. Mothers. The young children not chattering but stalled in mid-air like birds. First Uncle's five-year-old boy, my cousin Raven Sun, stretches his neck as if to follow his father. He knows that we will stand guard for weeks until they return. Wherever we are, gathering our nets full of flounder at low tide or curled up by the fire at night, we wait for them.

I will be a shell, empty, until my father and First Uncle return.

I might have stood until darkness, watching, had not Nana yanked my arm. She is breathless from running barefoot. Rushing down from the cliffs and her hideout there in her dress of Grandmother's red spun wool when she should have been here, saying goodbye. Down her back, her blue-black hair falls from up in the air in which it flew to hang at her waist. Since her birth, it has never been cut.

"Let's go up!" she yells. "You can see them turn on the currents and follow them until we have the light. It shines longer up there."

Already the water is dark. The canoes are specks. In just a moment of looking away, I can no longer tell which canoe is Father's. So I let her yank me away, like a fallen branch in her hands.

"It's late, Nana!" calls our mother, with a sharp edge in her voice, like bone needles. "Don't go up there. It is time to eat."

"Not hungry!" my sister yells back at her.

I see the frown on my mother's face, which I know will not soften until my father comes home. She turns away from the bold stares of the fish-wives. She must not disturb the air with angry words.

You will never tame Nana. She is the wind. I let her take me. Up. You can see the whole world from the cliffs, my sister says.

She has bird feet, this girl. She scales with her

bare toes gripping solid rock and her wide shoulders heaving herself up, as if she is made from feathers, not flesh. Up the ancient cliff-holds our ancestors once climbed, to the first cliff above the sea. Nana leads, although I was the one who taught her to climb.

We used to pretend we were ravens in our nests up there and caw at the village. Sometimes crows hung in the clouds above our heads, listening. But this evening we are silent. We flatten our bellies on the rock and look out.

Below, our family's Big House is closed to the sky, with a hole in the roof from which smoke curls. Twin totem poles, twenty feet high, guard the doorway. Surrounding it are many other plankhouses on a high bank. In the middle sits the Winter Ceremonial House. Dotting the sand in front of the village are red cedar totem poles. A carved raven sits on top of each pole, staring out with wide-open eyes, searching for enemies slipping past. War may come at any time, Father warns, revenge for blood Kwakiutls have spilled.

Out on the sea, the canoes form a vee, like geese returning in spring, the leader at their head. It is my father who will give the orders, be the first to step on Salish ground. He may be the first to fall. I want to confess this to Nana. Tell her there will be a lightning raid, a surprise attack on our enemies. The warriors will land in silence, tiptoeing with raised spears in the middle of the night, when all are

25

asleep. The cries of the dying will awaken the Salish. They will fight to the death. If I was there with them, I could shout warnings, be my father's shadow, battle beside First Uncle. Not one Kwakiutl would be taken.

But Nana's face is lit with the dying light. Her eyes shine with being up here, so high, away from the tribe. All alone. My sister has a secret life, one she lives apart from the rest of us. She doesn't know yet that I have changed with the departure of those canoes.

For now, I will lean over the cliff's edge with her. Let the wind blow my hair loose and wild. Close my eyes and feel the sea-salt air upon my skin. I will not tell her how I thirst to become that Raven warrior who will save our tribe.

These are the last of my winter days spent in a dreamspell with my sister.

CHAPTER 3

Walking with Grandmother

NANA

I did not say goodbye to Father yesterday. I know my mother would like to scold me for it. When I was young, I mourned at all his leave-takings, blackening my face as she did at war raids, fishing trips, and the tribe's long journey upriver. But my tears froze at the tribal gathering. I feared that just the sight of Father's painted face would make me scream out a warning.

Do not go! Do not kill the innocents!

That is what I would have said if I had waited down there on the sand with the women. I would have called him back. Back to safety and innocence. Back to when the Salmon Men grew undisturbed in their house beneath the sea. Back to when I trailed behind Father, awaiting his smile, his words of praise. The times I shone in his eyes.

Father will push the Way, and it will drench us all in blood.

Better to be perched on the cliffs, I thought. To find my own place apart from this village. Forget I am female. Unimportant. Nobody. Always alone, except for my oldest cousin. But years have passed since she left. No one mentions her name anymore. Certainly not my cousins, fast-moving boys, younger than me. Father forbids me to speak to the michimis except to give an order. There is only my brother to tell.

Last night Nanolatch and I watched until the moon rose high, long after the canoes vanished. Below us, Grandmother had roamed the shoreline long past dusk, staring out to sea. Finally we climbed down. As usual my brother rushed straight to the Big House to gulp his fish stew. My mother had saved it for him, still steaming on the fire. I ran to the beach to find Grandmother. She was the only one who could comfort those who watch and wait in this village. But she had vanished from the sand.

Light flickered from the Ceremonial House. I tiptoed near, hesitating in the doorway. A candle of eulachon burned inside. Grandmother knelt before the Twin Salmon totem poles carved by my great-great-grandfather. Their abalone eyes gleamed, like

the white underbellies of fish on moonless nights, as
if they still floated, remembering the dark underworld from which they came. In the flickering flame
the twenty-foot totem poles darkened to a blood red.
High upon the walls their shadows danced.

Grandmother's back was like a plank of wood—
rigid. Just her belly moved gently in and out. She
looked like neither man nor woman. Her face did
not seem hers, but that of another, before the wind
and sun carved those lines onto her face, before I
ever knew her. Perhaps she was speaking to the spirits, trying to eat up the evil.

I had no choice but to back away. Nowhere to go
but into the Big House. There is a hole at the bottom of the totem pole, an entrance, that is a carved
raven's mouth. The elders say when you pass inside
it, you are transformed. Through this I entered,
standing tall, unlike the adults who must bend. I
swallowed the remainder of the stew, bitter from
cooking so long. My mother watched me with dark
eyes, her cheeks and forehead sorrow-streaked with
ash. But she did not scold me. She patted my sleeping mat and I lay down without a word. She
smoothed my hair, combing its tangles with her
slender fingers.

Early this morning Grandmother paces the shoreline
in the endless drizzle as if she never slept. She is a
short woman, wide and full, like a salmon feeding
long years at sea. Her arms are raised to the skies,

whirling around, touching something invisible and drawing it down into her chest. Some say she should be shaman. But since Shilka became shaman, only men rule here.

Grandmother pauses when she hears my feet stir up the sand.

"You are a child of nature. So strong. You love those cliffs." She points upward. "I spy you up there most days, looking down, like you are the owner of the sea."

She takes my arm to steady her bare feet along the cool, wet sand.

"You will soon enter a time that will change you from a girl into a woman. I will ready you for your Initiation. Your mother will guide you too. Indeed, you have already begun."

Her face is full-moon bright as we walk along the beach.

"You climb like a warrior, facing fear. No other girl here can do that," she nods. "But you must learn to hear the spirits. For three years we will train you. At your Initiation you will leave the tribe and wait for your spirit guide to tell you the Way."

"Like Girl Who Is Gone?" I blurt out. I remember her. Her black hair glistening. Her face thin and startled. She was my oldest cousin, initiated at fourteen. So frightened was she to stay alone in the woods without her mother that she came running back, screaming. She met no spirit guide. For many moons, she wandered in a daze, jumping at the sound of the wind. Until her father, Second Uncle, traded her as a bride to a faraway tribe in the north. We never saw her again.

Grandmother shakes her head. "She had not learned to be stronger than her fear. She ran from the evil one who tested her and did not wait for a spirit helper. Her Initiation was not successful. Whatever you will be in life depends on what happens at that time."

"Couldn't someone have helped Girl Who Is Gone?"

"Old Dzonokwa appears to give girls courage. But the child was so held by fear, she didn't see the wild woman of the woods. If you stand your ground, you draw your spirit helper. Then evil vanishes."

"What if a girl is successful at her Initiation?"

"Some say if she is let loose from her Initiation, she is full of spirits. She could change the world with such power. Stop the sun. Pull the moon from the sky should she look at it. So Shilka demands that a girl hide for a length of time—from one new moon to the next." Grandmother frowns.

"What does she do then?" I wonder.

"When she returns, she begins a task. Weaving like your mother. Or becoming a gatherer of berries like your second cousin. She will marry a taise from another tribe."

I sift her words in my mind like grains of sand. Have a successful Initiation or fail, the end is the same for all Kwakiutl girls. We will marry some boy we did not choose and leave this village. A wish twists sharply in my belly—not to be born taise or even female, but to be male.

The gift of transformation belongs to males alone. Long ago, my grandmother said, Kwakiutls transformed themselves into animals to hide from their enemies. The animals taught them this secret, for they knew how to change into humans during a hunt. At the end of a chase, a warrior would find a beautiful maiden waiting instead of the deer he had been hunting.

I look out to sea where the fishermen canoe— dots against the frosty sky. Nanolatch is out there, gone at dawn. Later he will brag about the flounder caught, the size of the fattest one, and the tipping of the canoe with their weight. He wishes to be the first to spy the magical eulachon and run to tell the village. Eulachon are "salvation fish." When they run, winter ends.

How different Nanolatch and I are, although we are twins. I am round and smooth like a rock washed up from sea. Females sit long hours in the plankhouse like clamshells closed tight. But my brother is muscular like the salmon that push upstream from sea to mountain. He pulls in nets by the shore, his back bending like a willow branch that snaps up tall again. He never tires. If I were male, I'd fish by his side and do daring things—whip my flesh with a hemlock bough and plunge off the cliff into the deep sea.

Grandmother and I head to the Big House. Salty odors fill the air. The fishermen's wives brew a broth of clams and mussels, sweetened with blueberries. One by one the women gather for our midday meal. Afterward they set baskets of wool at their feet and spindles on their lap. Stillness settles over the plankhouse. My mother sits near the fire beside her loom. Long-limbed and tall, in her brown garment and long black braids, she still looks like a maiden. She calls me to her side.

"Nana, I worry about you. I don't say much. I keep waiting though."

I hold my breath and wait too.

"You are a chief's daughter. Born into wealth. I have let you roam free until now. But I have promised your father to ready you for your Initiation."

She smoothes the tangles in the bright yellow wool at her feet, separating each strand.

"Your brother will be trained at sea. You will learn here with me. No longer can you pretend and hide, as a child does."

Not once has she been to the cliffs with me, or seen the secret caves up there. Hundreds of them. I know them all. Footholds to crouch in, scaled by ancient warriors who dangled above the sea to carve them. Breathless high. If once my mother went there, she would always wish to go back, as I do.

Mother bends down to me. "I know you are full of joy up there. But you must soon give up your childhood games. After all your weaving is done,

you can climb in the late afternoon—until your
father returns."

She sits erect again, turning to her loom. I am
certain she does not wish to see my lips, drawn
down, as if I had licked salt out of the sea. I watch
her instead, pretending her fingers dive like swim-
mers in and out of the waves of wool.

After awhile she guides my fingers onto the
yarn. The rough strands refuse to slide in easily.

"Pay attention," she orders. "Still your mind."

I move closer, holding the yarn. My hands feel
like harpoons stabbing the wool. In and out I weave
the yellow thread, but it is lumpy beside my mother's neat stitches. There is no way to straighten it.
She yanks my threads out.

"She is not ready yet," Grandmother announces
from her spindle. "Her fingers are not strong. Next
year she will begin to weave. Let her help me
instead."

I almost run over to her like Yamunah, our dog,
when she is called. Sitting down at her feet, I pull
the white dog-hair from the baskets, unwinding it
into the air. My grandmother rolls it between her
palm and thigh, twisting it into a cord. She winds it
onto a spindle, spinning it down until the fur turns
into fine wool thread. Her face looks smooth when
she spins as if all her worries and her long years fly
away.

I wonder if I will smile at my work after my
Initiation and what my work will be. Already I am

restless from sitting. I can't get up and run off. From the looks of my mother's downcast mouth, I know I am expected to stay. It will be like this each afternoon if I don't hide. My head pulses. All I want is to run out to the beach and see if Nanolatch rides in. If only I could ride with him, dip the nets deep, and haul the day's catch in. But it is bad luck for a fisherman even to pass by a female as he goes to sea. It would scatter the fish in all directions, they believe, so none would remain to feed us. They would never allow a girl in their canoe, especially a chief's daughter.

The Way says a child must apprentice in her mother's work. So I must learn to collect weeds for dye and to comb, spin, and weave blankets. To be a weaver is to be an artist. That's what my mother is. She was born to it. She and weaving are one. I wonder if she found her place early, or if she ever questioned it as I do.

My mother and grandmother both have this knowing. I think my brother has this knowing too or he would not spend long hours at sea. They all sense something I do not.

Here is what I know— The men are gone. We are at war. Evil has been let loose. Yet the women do nothing but weave.

HERRING SPAWN MOON

NANOLATCH

The moon disappeared slice by slice, and for
nights the sky was black. Now it swells into
fullness again. Still they have not returned.
Above our heads this morning, heavy clouds
hang like fists. All is murky.
No sign.
What can this silence mean?
I set out to sea wildly, disobeying the fishermen in my canoe, grabbing a paddle from their
hands. Father said they alone should work, letting me drift like a child. I whoop war cries as I
ride, not caring if all the fish dash off. I try to
outpace the swift canoes of the tribal fishermen shooting past.
All I can think is that something happened to
our warriors. Father, the first to land.
Perhaps they had lain in wait for him. The
Salish may have spirits of their own to guide
them—dark devils. They may have fiercer
weapons than ours, although I heard only that
they are gentle and lazy. I wonder what the
tribe will do if our warriors do not return. Only
Shilka and the elders would be left to decide,
and none of them able to use a weapon.
If I was trained, I could set off after them.

Appear on the horizon with a dozen more
canoes and scare the Salish. Prop up frighten-
ing masks to show them our power. Dress in a
grizzly bear skin and roar across the water.
They would surely run from their battle and
leave the Kwakiutl safe.

The fishermen stop paddling at the edge of
the bay. The other canoes ride far out. My body
leans forward to follow them past the whitecaps to the deeper ocean. That's where the
prized halibut hide, the biggest fish. It's where
I rode with First Uncle dark nights ago. From
there, I could look southward to see if there is
any sign of the war party. I sit with my arms
across my chest and stare where I must not go
yet.

My canoe stops here. Father's orders.

The sea grows flat and still. Beside me, the
fishermen slowly drop traps at the end of long
cedar lines, into the water, to seek flounder.
The traps sink down, marked by buoys. Falling
farther down and down. Disappearing. We lean
like willows over the water, watching them
fall. Then we paddle along the shoreline, dropping more traps as we go. When at last the
traps are all down, we return to the first ones.
The fishermen yank each line to test it.

"Haul it in!" Head Fisherman yells. "It is
full."

We stretch back like trees in a windstorm.

The lines tug heavily in their hands. My legs hold firm to the boat's bottom. Even my chest swells. The trap finally rises, full of fish leaping, white bellied. Stuffed with flounder and sole, spring herring too. The catch is so heavy that, when the fishermen fill their arms with the fish, they fall back on top of us, laughing.

Slowly we scoop the catch from each trap into our cedar bark baskets, filling seven brimful. Head Fisherman smiles and passes the water sack around. The men lie back, squinting up at the sun that peeks through. Above our heads circle eagles and gulls. Seals squeal as they swim toward us, smelling fresh-caught fish.

I stretch out with the fishermen and sigh. Soon, Father promised, I will apprentice myself to First Uncle and become a warrior. Ride in his canoe far past the whitecaps. Ever since our midnight journey, I keep wondering when we will return there. He is the one who will give me my first harpoon, one that will pass through fire, touched by ancient blessings. I wonder if it will look like his, a cedar shaft carved with ravens—if it will be lean and sharp, with a hard bone point, and my aim as true. First Uncle has told me I will live at his hearth soon. If only the warriors' canoes appeared now, I could train with him.

I search again on the waters but see nothing.

The fishermen nudge me and I help them sink more traps down. Our canoe drifts lazily in circles. We shift away from the sea, turning toward shore where the michimis work. In the tidal sands fishwives dig clams. Their daughters gather seaweed and set it out to dry. From the plankhouses, smoke rises.

On the beach my sister and Grandmother walk, arm in arm. Always they are together, buzzing in one another's ears like sand flies. Grandmother's voice on the wind is as high pitched as a seagull's.

Hours later the sky gathers into fists. Layers of every shade of gray. Drabness brushed by streaks of slate and flecks of oyster shell. Dusk. The fishermen turn in from sea and we paddle beside them.

"Two halibut. Six of the fattest codfish you ever saw," they call in greeting.

"The boy hauls the lines in, pulling his own weight," the fishermen in my canoe boast. "Soon he will be as strong as us."

On shore the fishermen sort out their catch for the fishwives. The women lean their heads together, gossiping. The men tell fish tales and their wives laugh. You can tell today's catch is plentiful by listening to them bark like seals over their food. Finally the women decide that the largest codfish and halibut are to be dried. The rest will be used for a thick stew of halibut heads tomorrow. The main fishwife points out some fat flounder to bake over coals for our evening meal. The men slowly cart their catch away.

Beside me the fishwives' daughters are finishing their task too. Seaweed dangles over their forearms like long strands of rope. The girls are short and darkhaired, of all ages, some even older than I. A few laugh among themselves, whispering behind their hands at me. You can never know for sure what girls talk about, what makes them laugh like that. So light their voices on the air, almost like music. Their jet black eyes shining with secrets.

I shake my head at them, turning away from the beach.

But then the cries begin. Raven caws from the guard perched on the cliff, shrill and sharp. Hitting me like stone. Banging at my heart. All the fishermen rush back to the beach, their feet pounding on the sand. I spin around like wind. Face the haze of sky and sea.

War canoes on the horizon head straight toward us.

CHAPTER 4

The Sea Spills Blood

NANA

All the villagers gather at once. It's as if we were
one being, looking out with the same eyes. Three
returning war canoes appear, not an enemy, as we
feared. The fishermen set out in thin, swift canoes
to greet our warriors. Nanolatch and I splash after
them, but they fly past too furiously for us. We both
stand thigh deep in the sea, waves jumping to our
chest.

My brother peers through the smoky air, counting the warriors who stand.

"Sixteen less than cast off," he pants. "No sign
of Father."

Shilka arrives, herding the slaves. Half-naked,

heads down, they cluster together with their drums. They beat, banging hard and slow. They pump a rhythm of fear and sorrow. It quickens my heart. Surely our warriors will hear the pounding out there and know that our hearts beat, waiting for them.

"There!" Nanolatch points. "Father is standing!"

The guard spills out his raven cries again to let us know the chief is safe. Short squawks, they cut the air, calling everyone's attention. The villagers raise a mighty roar. My breath flies back into my chest.

The elders reach the beach, stumbling behind on their staffs. Grandmother walks slowly with them.

My mother shouts when we spy Father. She had waited for him—darting her eyes out to sea every hour, black ash lines etched on her cheeks—her mouth seemingly stuffed with mussel shells. She had not even scolded me for disappearing each afternoon when I should have been spinning. But when Father's canoe is sighted, she rushes back to the Big House. She will cleanse her face of mourning ash, then plait her braids before she runs down, breathless to greet him.

When the warriors touch shore, my brother drags their canoes in with the fishermen. We search each face for the ones who are missing. The warriors' mouths are flat. They do not lift their heads even when their own children slip a hand into theirs, claiming them. Their spears and clubs lay forgotten in the canoes, not raised high above their heads. Not one war cry do we hear among them.

We surround the canoes. One is loaded with furs—booty from the Salish and a strange bundle of hair and bare flesh, someone all curled up. But in the other two canoes, fourteen warriors lie flat, unmoving, wrapped from head to toe in bark so that we cannot see their faces. One warrior lies apart, uncovered. The children flock around them. Their mothers gasp and fall to their knees.

Then I hear the wailing.

Grandmother collapses in the sand beside the canoe. "My son! I have lost you. Another one!"

It is First Uncle who lies stretched out, as if sleeping. His eyes are closed and his mouth open as if gasping for one last breath. On his bare chest is a dark opening of flesh, the blood seeping out, turning black.

"The Salish fought hard and so did we." Father's voice is a whisper, not his voice at all. "But one of their arrows was poisoned and hit First Uncle. We hurried back, hoping to heal him. He left us moments ago."

My brother drops down beside First Uncle. His chin quivers, holding his tears in. Beside him, Raven Sun trembles, his face pale and flat as sand.

"He thought he would make it back to you." Father touches each boy's shoulder. "The others died fast. But he held on. To die in sight of his home."

Everyone kneels in the sand. The stillness of the dead warriors fills us. Time stops. All we hear is

Grandmother, beating the drum that is her chest.
And the waves pounding in, a deafening pause
between, and their roar again like a storm's breath.
We stand an endless time.

Finally Shilka raises his staff. "We will honor the
warriors. They will rest tonight, guarded in the Ceremonial House. Tomorrow we will set them in our
burial grounds. But tell me, Chief, did we avenge the
salmon and save the seas?"

"We killed those Salish on the coast." Father
flings his words like fouled food. "They will fish the
sea no more."

Shilka nods to the fishermen to carry the fallen
warriors to the Ceremonial House. The rest of the
villagers surround Father and Shilka in a wide circle,
watching the chief greet us. He steps first to my
mother. She wears her best garment, a white woolen
robe with salmonberries embroidered onto its hem.

"How beautiful you are, my wife," he tries to
smile.

"Husband, I have waited for you in quietness.
Daring not to disturb the spirits. My time has been
used well. Two salmon swim on my blanket. You
will see it when you enter the Big House."

Father sighs heavily, frowning at Shilka. My
mother's stillness and all her steady weaving have
not saved our warriors. Beside us, Grandmother is
silent now. I help her to her feet but she sways from
side to side. Father orders two commoners to stand
beside her, one on each side, should she faint.

He turns to Nanolatch next, surrounded by a few fishermen. He gives one of them permission to speak.

"Your son has fished with us every day in the bay. He pulls more than half a man's share at sea."

My father beams. He places his hands on my brother's shoulders.

"I set you a test, son. To stay in the bay. Not to go farther, as you would have liked, but to obey the fishermen. You have passed this test. Now that you have done this, you are ready."

Nanolatch gasps. "But, how can it happen, without—?"

"We have lost fifteen of our best warriors. Only a handful remain to protect us. Some are wounded. You must start your training now. Tomorrow you will fish in Second Uncle's boat and stay by his side."

The Ceremonial House suddenly brightens with light. My brother turns toward it. He has no thought of training. He would rather be alone with his favorite uncle now. It will be the last time he will see him. But Nanolatch is not free to go yet. Father does not dismiss us.

His eyes are on me now. Already I tremble. When I was a young child, I met him eye to eye. I could always make him laugh. But now he keeps his distance. He speaks only to give me an order.

"I have spoken to our friends, the Nootkas, daughter," he nods. "We have made plans for you.

But first, I must see that you are ready."

He and my mother exchange glances. The Nootkas are a tribe from beyond the land, where my mother came from. She lowers her eyes to the sand. My heart quickens. Beneath my feet, the beach shifts like quicksand.

"How is Nana's weaving?" he asks my mother.

"She came..." She bites her lip.

I came twice to her side and then I disappeared for good.

Grandmother pulls away from the michimis. She holds her hand up flat. "Nana needs one more year. She can spin with me until then."

"If I put her to the test right now," demands my father, "could she at least thread yarn and follow a pattern?"

My grandmother reaches out for me. "She is still a child."

"Even a child must follow the Tribal Way," his voice tightens.

The villagers stand still. I squirm from one foot to another as if the sand burned. Father can decide anything he wants and I must do it. That was what happened to Girl Who Is Gone. I feel Father's anger flame like fire. He looks out to the cold gray sea, as if trying to calm himself.

"We passed by the rim of the ocean. I heard the salmon mourning there," he says. "The Tribal Way is broken. The deaths of the Salish are not enough. Each of us must be careful to follow the Way and atone for those who do not."

My mother bows her head. "What would you have the girl do?"

"I order her to spend each afternoon weaving. If she needs a guard to see that she comes, I will send one."

Behind him, we hear a stirring. All the canoes have been emptied and dragged off. Except one. A warrior shoves a strange creature out of that canoe and sends it flying face down into the sand. He yanks it by the back of the head, slicing his spear through her thick, waist-long hair.

"A slave for you." Father surprises my mother.

My mother stares at this creature—a Salish girl crouched into a ball, a knot of arms and legs. A scrap of cedar bark covers her. Strands of bloodied hair hang in her face. Tattoos are stamped across her cheeks in odd patterns. She is just a child, probably not much older than me.

"I don't have use for a slave," she pleads. "My work is something I create alone. This slave would only interfere with me."

"But I brought her back for our family's use," insists Father.

My mother pauses.

"Let Nana have her," my mother tells him. "My daughter wanders everywhere where I cannot follow. I fear she will scale the top cliffs soon, pretending she is a boy. She needs a companion to watch her."

In the moment she says it, her hand flies to her

mouth. She gasps but it is too late. Every single person in the village is standing there on the beach, and they all hear.

I am disobedient. Unruly. Lazy. I do not follow the Way. Red patches spread over my face.

Father scowls, motioning to his warriors. "Train this slave for wood gathering and fire keeping. Then she can trail our daughter. Nana cannot roam wherever she pleases. No longer will I allow her to climb those dangerous cliffs."

Grandmother bends down to the creature. She lifts the slave's chin. Around her neck is a deerskin necklace strung with grizzly bear claws. The villagers gasp. Even the fishermen step back. It is the sign of a supernatural one—a shaman.

Shilka pokes the slave with his staff. "This one is nothing. Too young to be initiated. Probably stole that necklace. The Salish are sly. We must watch her and train her to serve us as a slave."

"What shall we call this Salish girl?" Grandmother asks. "If she belongs to Nana, it is Nana's right to name her."

Second Uncle spits. "Call her nothing. She is a ghost."

I don't want this slave. She will betray me, replacing my own shadow. But then I remembered when I was young I had a shadow friend. She was an invisible one, who followed behind me without my ever seeing her. I alone believed she was there. I thought if I just stopped short and twirled around

one day, I would see her face to face. But I never did.
Noh was her name.

I mutter it aloud, "Noh!"

Second Uncle nudges the girl with his foot, kick-
ing her toward me. She creeps on all fours like a dog,
strings of short wild hair in her face, panting instead
of breathing.

"Find wood, ghost." Second Uncle points to the
driftwood on the sand and then to me. "Sleep at
Nana's feet. Never let her out of your sight."

The slave's eyes are spiritless. She does not hear
or see us at all.

None of us eat that night. We must fast until the
burning of the Dead. That is the Way. We kneel in
the Ceremonial House where the warriors stretch
out flat, facing the sky. First Uncle rests, clothed in
soft elk robes. Black raven feathers are sprinkled
upon him. His harpoon lies across his still chest. I
feel the air swirling like currents of wind in a storm,
a sign of his Spirit rising. At midnight, the tribe
leaves. Only the taises remain, as is our right, for
the long sleepless night ahead.

Grandmother reaches first for the sacrificial
knife that gleams near the fire. She slices through
her thick gray braid, sawing it away. Her fallen braid
drops down beside First Uncle. My mother screams
when she does this, setting a chill all through me.
Then Father grabs the knife. The blade whirs
through the air. In one split second, his long black

hair falls to the sand. Only adults, those who have been initiated in the Raven Clan, can do such a thing. But first, mourning must rip at their heart and make them wish for death.

The taises sit up, straight-backed. Nanolatch does not budge. I cannot look upon him. He hangs his head as if he has lost everything. My father's shadow rises high above the dead warriors. It hovers above me. A warning. An order. All the places I can't go anymore. Something chokes in my throat, making me want to cough. But I dare not disturb the deathwatch.

I press against the wall, wishing for sleep, sweet forgetfulness. Noh crouches nearby, her eyes flashing like flames in the darkness. Her name fits. Noh shall be my shadow. Because she is nothing, more ghost than human, lower than a michimi, she will stay with me.

WITHOUT A SPIRIT

Noh

I awake in the dark and find the shell that is me on the beach. An outcast. Screeching. Alone. Flinging a voice I never had—a wail, wrenched from somewhere deep in my belly, across the sea. Southward. To my home, where the sea mists rolled in, thickening the air. The one mountain, snowy white even in summer, sometimes hidden beneath a ring of clouds for days. The same sunless sky. The same wild sea.

Pressed down flat in the Kwakiutl canoe, kicked into a corner, I lost my voice. I tried to call out to the ones left behind, but no words came. No memory. I lay in a dark place between this world and the Spirit World, full of clouds. The canoe sped on but I stepped into a shadowy place. The spirits of the Salish swirled there, screeching death cries, caught by surprise, drenched in their own blood. All the ghosts in my village roamed loose with no one to bury them.

My mother's face appeared, white as morning fog. She reached out her hands to me. I thought she would lift me up out of that canoe and take me with her on her ghost journey. I rose to follow her. But she disappeared like mist blowing out to sea. Around my neck, I felt a tightening, a heavy weight. I fell back into my body with a thump.

I did not know who I was anymore. Bone. Flesh. A skeleton. My breath kept pushing my lungs in and out. I did not will it or tell it to do these things. I begged instead, Let me die! I could hear my heart pound and I didn't understand why. I was forever changed.

It wasn't until I heard the salmon wail that I

knew where we were. We passed by the
Salmon House where the fish mourn. Their
deep-throated cries ripped me apart.

Death is everywhere, I thought—even out
there, in the middle of the ocean.

It was then I remembered. There were no
women anywhere. When I turned around, they
had all vanished, my younger brother and sisters too. The children had gone without a
sound. That was the worst of it. After the
fierce screaming, all that silence.

I was on the shoreline with my father when
the angry words broke out. The Kwakiutl warriors had landed so swiftly, lifted in on wind
and tide as if the spirits flew with them. I ran
for Father's spear and carried it back to him,
but he was already down on the sand, his heart
pierced and blood pumping from his chest. One
last word he mouthed to me before the blood
gushed there too.

Run!

But the sand spun and the longhouses
danced, and I felt like I was spinning out to
sea.

I must stop. I don't want to remember. I will
be a mussel shell—glued tight with my own
juices. Nothing will pry me open.

I shall not.

I shall not.

I shall not ever speak to them.

CHAPTER 5

Churning

NANOLATCH

On the afternoon of the burning, we abandon First
Uncle and the warriors in the burial grounds. They
stretch flat on endless planks raised high in the air.
Never have so many died at once. The whole village
watches. Father hurries me away so I will not witness
the end of it—Uncle turned completely into ash.

"Let the women stay," he orders. "They will
guard the Dead."

He urges me to break my fast for the long day
ahead. I am not hungry but I eat, as all the men do. I
stumble out of the Big House, my insides screaming.
Too soon we canoe where the whitecaps toss, where
I always begged to go. Only he is not with me. Ten

fishermen cast off with Second Uncle and me. Father stays behind, drumming in a circle with Shilka, some wounded warriors and the elders.

The wind picks up and a sheet of charcoal gray hides half the sky. A spring storm brews. The sea churns. Raindrops spit at our heads. Our canoe knifes through the water with the swells, up and down, throwing me from side to side. Words and cries whirl inside me, like I am the eye of the storm. I squeeze tight to the bow and scarcely breathe until we stop. In the kelp beds, the men tie the canoe to the plants to hold us still.

We call the halibut. My job is to tie bait on the bone hooks. A raven carving—the sharp-eyed one who sees everywhere, even beneath the dark sea— marks each hook. Fat octopus meat wiggles in my fingers as I slide it on. Sweet food, the fishermen smile. They dip long cedar lines with seal stomach buoys into the sea. Down and down the lines sink. The men sing to the fish, calling names to lure them. Old Squint-Eye, they croon. I almost laugh.

"Perhaps even now they have stopped," Head Fisherman says. "Far below us they listen."

So the men chant, calling the halibut yet another name.

Now come, Old Woman!
Now you have enough to eat!
Now you have tasted our sweet food!

The boat rocks back and forth. Nothing stands still. The sky flips over. Everything spins. I retch my meal, my face touching the waves. A fisherman grabs the back of my hair, heaving me up. On the canoe's bottom, I pant like a dying fish. Second Uncle narrows his eyes at the sight of my pale face.

No one coaxes me up. No one breathes strength into me the way First Uncle would have done with just a look. I won't budge. I refuse to fish. When we head back that evening, I set my feet on the sand and run.

The first few days go like that. Until the embers die.

Far out to sea, we could still see the swirling streaks of smoke that were our warriors burning. Black at first. Thick. Then misty gray. Wisps. The scent of burnt flesh no longer in the air.

I grit my teeth and bait as I am told. But I do not sing to the fish. Every time I try to speak, it chokes me. I follow Second Uncle's commands silently.

On the fourth day, just as the sun sinks, the buoys bounce up and down. A huge halibut thrashes on the line below. The fishermen let it yank this way and that. When at last it grows quieter, they haul in the rope. Three men lift up Old Squint-Eye. Another three lean out to club its head, bringing it quick death. The halibut fills the bow.

On the trip back to shore, in the shallow water, I trail my fingers in the water. A school of silvery fish run by. Eulachon! I grab a net, lean far out, and capture six in one dip. It has been a good day at last. We are rewarded by spring's salvation fish. We have longed all winter for its rich taste in our mouths. The first ones caught are roasted whole. Mostly their oil is drained, then dribbled over plain flounder, making it crisp. I know what the fishwives will do when they spy eulachon in our baskets. They will grin widely, smacking their lips, showing their gums. They will cluck like birds with a worm.

But when we land, I, who always yearned to be the first to shout out about the eulachon, let a fisherman yell it. And the fishwives come running. But not my sister.

Where has she disappeared? No sign of her these last few days since Father's orders fell like a slap upon her face. There is nowhere to hide, no cliff to run to, that will stop the Way.

In the Big House, when I come in for the evening meal, Nana sits with a pouting face, Yamunah in her lap. Fur covers her garment. I yank her braid but she won't look up.

Father questions the fishermen at once. "How did my son do today?"

The first few days, he was greeted by silence. Frowns. Downcast eyes. No one wanted to tell him I am still a boy, my stomach tossing like waves, not used to the wildness of the sea.

"The boy baits swiftly," they boast that evening. "Spied the eulachon before any of us did. Some of us will now go to the mouth of the river to harvest them. When we return, the Chinook salmon should begin to run. Soon we will all fish upriver."

The fishermen slap one another on the back. Their laughter bounces around the plankhouse, banging in my ears. They sit around the fire-pit with Father and Second Uncle, telling fishing stories long into the night. They speak of salmon running upriver, jamming it shoulder to shoulder, top to bottom. How the sun scorches the ones on top while those on the bottom rip their flesh on rock. They say you can stand in the mountains and hear salmon flipping on the water a long distance downstream.

I wonder where these men store their grief. They bury it so deeply that you cannot read it on their faces. Sorrow sank right through my heart, heavy as rock. I have waited my whole life to train as a warrior, and suddenly I am not ready. First Uncle was the brother of my father and Second Uncle. Yet already they turn away from him.

As I must too.

I slip outside and climb straight to the burial grounds where all is silent. Against the sky the planks rise high in the air. First Uncle's ashes have smoked everywhere these last few days. I have not been allowed to shed one tear. But now, in the dark, they fall by themselves. I do not want Uncle's spirit to see me like this. My feet run before I tell them to.

There is nowhere to be alone except the beach.

I crouch behind a totem pole. Lean my face against its carved flesh, the woodsy scent so familiar.

Cedars that once lived—that dug roots into the
earth—stand like bare bone, stripped of their bark
skin. I rub my hands over them, feeling the scar
holes where once their branches grew.

Cries heave from my gut. I no longer know who I
am with this pain, never felt before, burning through
me. Never imagined that one, whose eyes I have
looked into since I was born, is not here anymore.
Those deep brown eyes knew me best. He saw each
layer of my soul, naming places I had no words for.

Grandmother insists First Uncle is everywhere.
But I can't find him. When the smoke died down,
when his ashes lifted to the wind, he was gone.

When I finally look up, it is to find Noh standing
near the shoreline with her back to me. She no
longer crawls on all fours as she did the first week.
Father has ordered her to stand up like the rest of the
slaves. She follows our commands, but never speaks
one word. From a distance, she watches us, her eyes
sorrow-dark.

She surprises me for she is taller than the girls
here. Her short hair blows in the breeze like tangled
seaweed. She is narrow and lean like a fish skeleton,
her skin bark browned.

When she first landed, I saw her hair first. Thick
and raven-dark, it blew around her like wings, as if
she flew here to tell us something. But, close up, I
saw bruises all over her legs and arms from Second
Uncle's foot and how her eyes darted wildly. When
the warrior's spear cut through her long, rustling

hair, to mark her as our slave, I held my breath. So close to her neck it sliced, I thought he would kill her. I tried to swell my body, become a boulder, cover the sight of our Big House rising behind me.

I did not want her to guess that it was where four slaves once went, one sunk into each corner post as the house was built years ago. It was an honor, my father told them, before the spear sliced through their heads. The remaining slaves watched, all in a line, wondering who would be next.

Slaves are nothing, I was taught. But this one never was a michimis. Like a silent totem pole, she stares out to sea, in a world of her own. The necklace remains around her neck. No one dared remove it. Even Shilka would not touch it. Perhaps he was afraid it would burn his hands.

This is a girl who has lost her whole tribe. One who must live voiceless, her head bowed, her day a string of commands. What can it be like to let everyone go and never see them again? I can taste it now. I have never been a moment without First Uncle.

I wonder why such a girl, one of no power, stirs me.

THE WATCHER

NOH

The boy weeps. The burial grounds are full of ash, and it is dark, so dark. No one is outside except us two. I do not think he sees me but I hear him. Without even turning around, I know it is Nanolatch. He had lingered in the gravesite, stumbling, not sure of his step. He who is so strong, his back straight and muscled, crying.

I am still, listening.

I have been so numb. I could not cry since losing Father and all my village. I stand there after his cries stop and he is long gone. I still hear it, let it pour through me like rain, touching the wounds I keep hidden from my conquerors. Something rises inside me like the sun, stretches wide open in the new warmth. My sorrow feels the brush of soft sea air. Once again I see the mountain beyond my home, frosty white in the distance.

Something stirs inside me. I, who drifted in the Land of the Dead so long I felt like a ghost, am alive again. Death's spell begins to lift from me.

Only the scars remain. Hollow places with the names of my father Fire Holder. My mother, the shaman, called Wind Tamer. My brother, Dancing Bear. Sisters, Gift from the Clouds and Red Cod Running. Never to be seen again.

Afterward I crawl into the smoky house to curl up by the girl's feet, pulling the dog to me. That is the spot they gave me. I watch the girl's round sleeping face: she has never felt grief like mine. She is offered a soft life, dreaming and weaving

by the fire, but she turns her face from it. And
I, who have lost my mother and who had hopes
of becoming a shaman like her, will have no
future.

Perhaps I should hate Nana for that.

But what stops me from hate is the undercur-
rent that runs through the girl, the sadness
that is river-bottom deep. She is like a fish
caught and flung to shore. On the sand she
thrashes, breathless. She chokes on cold sea
air.

Their faces are the same; their ways so different. The boy sparks this churning inside me.
Something calls me to them both, as if I knew
them from some past place.

The girl is full of secrets. Who she is, I want
to find out, and where she belongs. I have
guessed her hiding spot, a forbidden place. I
know to creep up slowly so she won't hear me.
Slip beneath some bushes that dare to grow on
the cliffs, unseen from below. Who does she
speak to up there?

I will follow her everywhere. I will never let
her out of my sight. But it is not because they
order me to do it.

I hang in the air beneath her.

CHAPTER 6

Traveling with the Spirits

NANA

At the first pause, when the flames die down, I slip away. Nowhere to breathe in this smoggy place, except as high up as I can climb, where the air is clear, looking down over the water. I search for a sign, for the warrior who will eat up the evil. I hide from all the plans Father says he has for me, pressed flat down, so no one could guess I hide there.

From here I spy the man we call Spiritless One, roaming on the sand below. He gives me shivers although he is a safe distance away. Grandmother says he once looked upon Sisiutl, the great sea monster. Afterward his soul drifted with the wind, leaving behind his body like an empty seashell. The body is just a cloak, Grandmother says. Only the soul gives it life.

Though I fear to look upon him, I can't help staring. Part of me drifts too. Something is missing. The girl I once gave to Father is gone and I don't know where she went. I must do just what he says. Follow his way. Not find my own way.

I do not worry about such things for long because the cliff begins to shake beneath me. Footsteps dig into the rock. That slave girl must have seen me running from the village. In no time, she pulls herself up and crouches on her heels to watch me. Her gaze seems bold. Bright beetle eyes she fixes on me as if she knows everything.

"Go away!" I point downhill. "Go back down!" Inch by inch she crawls toward me. I lift my chin in the air, ignoring her. I study the ocean's waves. Closer she creeps. The scent of seaweed and sweat from her unwashed skin makes my nose wrinkle. Then the annoying one waves her arms in my face and points down. There is a blur far below, by the burial grounds. A figure waves to me. Grandmother! I had forgotten my promise to apprentice myself to her, to learn the ways of the Dead.

I rise so quickly that it startles Noh. She falls back onto the rock. The slave had only come to bring a message, nothing else. If she were a person, I could say I was sorry.

I hurry down while she descends slowly behind. Noh does not follow me out of the village where the

Dead roam. In front of the grounds the slave crouches, screeching as if she has stepped on fire. She flattens her body to the sand. She stares at the burial grounds as if something has moved there. Not one living warrior even dares to visit us. Grandmother and I are quite alone. Only women work to soothe the newly Dead—to calm them so they do not haunt our village or seek revenge.

In the burial grounds, all is ash-gray. Burned down bodies stretch high above us, resting under the sky. I hold my breath, listening.

"Have the spirits left?" I look around.

She shakes her head of cropped gray hair. "First we must mourn the lives gone too soon, and the pain in which they died. After a time, if we honor the Dead, their Spirits will dance. Peace will come."

We must visit them each day, she says. She instructs me to fill baskets brimful with sweet cool water from the spring. Spread fresh cut cedar around the planks to cleanse the evil that grabbed my uncle. We cook special food, my uncle's favorite—crisp smelts fried to a crunch. Food for his journey back and forth from the Country of the Ghosts. Where the Dead feast and tell stories and see us still. Until he leaves us, bit by bit, tiring of the distance.

"I want to know how I can recognize the spirits," I beg her.

She watches the sea beyond the fishermen's canoes. I know she waits for a sign—the passage of the migrating ones. Come spring, if you look closely, you might see sprays of water shooting up. It is the whales breathing. She tells me a story then.

There is always a story.

Once, when she was young, she drifted in a canoe after her Initiation trial. The sea suddenly grew still. A whale swam beside her. She whispered to it, calling its spirit as her grandmother had taught her. From out of the blowhole appeared a round face, like the moon, with its eyes upon her.

"I felt it watching me as if it knew me. Time stopped. The canoe floated. I was not afraid. When the whale swam away, I was changed. I was no longer a young girl."

"What happened to you, Grandmother?"

"From then on, I could see into the world. Stand on shore and know that the eulachon swim twenty miles away. See the future before it happens. It gives me great strength because I know the spirits are always with me."

"But how will I know them?" I worry. "You still haven't told me."

"You will be filled with light. No darkness will dim it. The Way will be certain. There will be no doubt."

I sigh deeply. That is something I have never felt. Nothing is certain for me. Everyone tells me what they wish me to do. Weave this. Dye that. Stay here. If only I knew what I could be. I should stuff my ears with sand so I will not hear what my parents demand of me.

Grandmother begins to chant, rocking back and forth as she stands beneath my uncle's ashes. I join my voice with hers. The damp air rings with our song.

Let your spirit fly now.
We have fed you and warmed you.
Go back to the country from where you came.

Words have power, Shilka says. Words slice through the veil between this world and that of the spirits, if you sing with a pure heart. The chanting drowns all the voices in my head so I only think of soothing First Uncle and the dead warriors.

When I open my eyes, the gloom lifts a moment. A ray of brightness shines, cleansing our sorrow. The spirits must be pleased. For it could only be them that brushed my heart just now. I help Grandmother set out the evening meal for the fallen warriors. At dusk she gathers her cedar cape tightly around her shoulders and heads toward the plankhouses.

I climb back to the cliffs. No one would guess I come in the dark. My duties keep me busy all day. Just now Noh is feeding the fire, so she can't spy on me. I will not let that creature come up. She doesn't belong here. This is the last place that is mine before my Initiation. I want my childhood to stretch out forever, like the sea below me.

There is light even so late, once your eyes get

used to it. In that light I pick my way. When I am ready to go back down, the stars will pop out to guide my steps. As I climb, I remember my mother nagging me one afternoon while I spun wool. She knows I still climb, even though it is forbidden. But she is content, trusting Noh to trail me.

"Why do you go up there? You could run along the beach or play in the forest, but you always climb the cliff instead."

"It just calls me and I go," I shrugged.

"If you should slip and fall, it is a long distance down. Not even Shilka's power will heal you."

"My feet are tough," I said. "I know the right spots to hold onto."

She should see me now, edging my way up in the dark.

At the top, I sweep my eyes down to the village. Below, Nanolatch pauses in the burial grounds. But he can't hear the ringing on the misty air or feel the wings of the spirits touch down. I don't think he can hear the Dead. Not many males can. No one is like my grandmother, who hears all the world stirring.

Better to be up here, alone. Far from my chores and the slave who would surely betray me now. Apart from my brother, who must find his own Way through pain, as Grandmother teaches. Hidden from Father, so I do not feel the barriers, as if a whole forest grew between us.

I can still hear my mother questioning me.

I scaled it early, when I was barely six, following

Nanolatch. But even before I could walk, I had always looked up to the cliffs, wanting to see. "What is out there?" My mother would press me to explain.

I look far out to sea. I have never been there. No one has. No one can ever go there in human form. You must be transformed to visit there. The Country Beyond the Ocean is out there, where the Salmon Men live deep below the sea. Perhaps they grow there now, forgiving what has been done to them, their mourning song dimmed. If only they sent their own warrior to atone. To break this spell.

It seems brighter out there on the water, like the first star shining in the evening sky. It is spring, I coax them. The eulachon run. Surely the salmon feel the current calling them upriver.

Below me, the whole village holds their breath and waits for the first spring salmon—the Chinook—to return, the biggest of them all.

GHOST DANCE

NOH

How they hiss when they see me on the beach. Fourteen shapes shift like fog, roaming between Grandmother and the girl in the burial grounds. Ghosts pound their fists at me. They fling their arms above their heads to toss imaginary spears at the sand.

They shout, "Kill! Kill all of them!"

The newly Dead push fiercely at the border
between the burial grounds and the village,
between the Dead and the living, trying to
break free. If they get loose, they will blow
everywhere like fog. Up and down the coast,
they will roam through all the villages, seeking
revenge.

This is a haunt, where the restless Dead do
not sleep.

Grandmother lays down gifts. Fried smelts.
Cool spring water. She waves branches of burning cedar. It crackles, smudging the air with
musty wood smoke. She pushes these smoke
clouds toward the warriors. They turn from
me, becoming quiet. They gather around her as
if warming themselves around a campfire.
Chants brighten the air. The ghosts soon forget
me, for Flies on Wind has cast a spell on them.
One by one, the warriors yawn and drop their
spears. A single warrior points to the planks.
The Dead march off and climb onto their
planks to sleep.

I am almost ready to run off when that one
warrior steps toward me. He is the tallest one,
their leader perhaps. I can see through his
body. Black paintings on his chest waver in the
air. He rises out of the ground like mist, waving something of cedar and bone, a shadow har-

poon. This must be Nanolatch's First Uncle, the one whose deathwatch we kept my first night here. He does not stomp like the others or writhe in pain, as they did. At the edge of the burial grounds, he stops.

Nearby, the girl scowls at me, yet continues at her tasks, noticing nothing. Grandmother looks straight at me, nodding her head. Her chants have put the warriors to sleep. And still she sings. As long as she says the soothing words, First Uncle can step no farther.

His eyes are charcoal circles, and his face is so gray I almost pity him. My heartbeat slows. I have no fear to look upon this ghost. The Dead visited me once before in that speeding Kwakiutl canoe. I know such a thing is possible.

Salish shamans, like my mother, spin spells to keep the tribe safe. But some shamans have the gift of seeing, my mother said. To them come visions—pieces of the past or future to puzzle over, things that come from the spirits to point the way. Such shamans can see the ghosts of the Dead walking, and hear their words.

This gives me courage to speak up. "What do you want?" I whisper.

I crawl close. Soon his words come, but not of his mouth. They whirl in my mind like wind.

I pity the boy. He and I had a pact.
"What was it?" I ask.
To train Nanolatch. Give him my harpoon.
Send my power into him. He was born to do
great deeds.
"What deeds?"
To be the greatest fisherman and leader.
More I cannot tell you. But he cannot become
who he is supposed to be unless I touch him.
He holds out his hands to me, palms of see-
through clouds. Useless.
I have no power in your world anymore, but
you do!
"What...can I do?"
Shivers creep up and down my body. I squat
here with my hands and feet digging into the
cold, wet sand, and yet speak to a ghost. I am
just a girl, a shaman's daughter, yes, but I did
not yet have my Initiation. I have no guardian
spirit. There is so much to learn. All I wanted
was to be trained by my mother.
I want to enter the boy's spirit. I could do it
through you. You are a shaman. You alone
have this gift. Let me help the boy through
you.
Then I remembered my mother, Wind Tamer,
telling me how ghosts can be clever, pulling
you into their sorrow so you no longer live in
this world but roam in the Spirit World with
them. When I was captured in that Kwakiutl

canoe, I had longed to return to the dead Salish. I was spiritless. Although I had a body, I had no strength to fight back. I should have tossed myself overboard and swam back home instead.

Ghosts are to be controlled, my mother taught. Don't let them take over, she warned.

First Uncle thinks I am a shaman. But I am not one. Yet.

I look straight into the dead warrior's eyes. "If I do this thing you ask, give you the boy, you must do what I tell you."

He nods.

I point to the sleeping shapes on the planks.

"Keep them here in these grounds. Never let them set foot in this village or any other place. Only you can leave."

I will obey you, Noh.

Long he lingers, looking through me. Then he trudges wearily toward his plank. But he does not sleep like the others. He stares up at the stars as if he lives among them.

I crouch alone on the sand, trembling. This ghost asks me to be a link, to step between the living and the Dead, the space between the boy and him.

A no-man's land, where I have not stepped before.

CHAPTER 7

Moon of the Salmon

NANOLATCH

A fire of alder wood smolders on the sand all spring. Smoke drifts far out to sea. Shilka dances on the beach. Onto his bare flesh, fish scales are etched in charcoal. His face hides beneath a mask of blackened wood with red figures leaping all over it. When he shakes his head, his white hair flies in the wind. It reaches past his waist in a tangle of knots and twigs.

The shaman lifts his staff to test the wind and studies the clouds for hours. He speaks to the souls of the salmon, listening for their splashing upriver. It is he who will decide when the fishermen will travel to fish there. You can hear him chanting to the salmon everywhere in our village. All the tribe listens, pausing at their tasks.

But the Moon of the Salmon shrinks and still the Chinook do not run. Another moon rises and falls. The fishermen drag their canoes out to sea to catch codfish. Then the rains come late. Days of heavy downpour force the fishermen to huddle inside with the weaving women.

One night Shilka dances late into dark upon the soggy sand. His voice drones on and on. Something changes in his step. Eyes closed, he weaves from side to side. Suddenly, he is not dancing but curving everywhere. Like a fish, he swims across the sand, fighting invisible waves.

We have already settled by the fire-pit for the night when the shaman enters, standing in the door-way, inside the raven's mouth. Everyone looks up at him. Grandmother smiles, as if she knew all.

"The salmon are splashing! A sound so faint, it can hardly be heard. Some have turned into the river and head upstream," he announces. "It is time to leave for upriver."

Everyone stirs. My cousins, half-asleep, nudge one another and sit up. Raven Sun rushes to my side. The fishwives cackle with excitement. My sister leans toward Shilka, her eyes shining. She is not allowed to speak or question him. Only males can.

"Who will travel there this time?" I demand.

Shilka frowns because someone dares ask a question. The young are taught to learn by watching and waiting. But I stare boldly at the shaman, snapping my fingers. All heads turn. The chief's son asks and it is his duty to answer.

"The twins will go from now on," he answers. "Your presence will be a totem for us. It will let the salmon know that we are one with them."

I hear my sister gasp. She will be in utter ecstasy there. There will be someplace new for her to discover. She will run around to seek new hiding places.

"How long will we stay upriver?" I ask.

"As long as the salmon run. Perhaps some Chinook first, then sockeye. Until midsummer," Father says. "From birth to death, we follow them."

I sigh with contentment. It sounds like forever. I lean into my sister, pushing my weight against her shoulder. She presses back into me. We will be free there. She will not have to spin inside all the long hours. I will not have Second Uncle's eyes constantly upon me, noticing my small failures. I have never felt like this before. I have been an arrow striking my target. I have always obeyed. But I want to be as full of flight as my sister.

On the dawn of our departure, the fishermen heave twelve canoes into the sea, heading north. A few slaves travel with us, bound together, back to back. My sister spits upon the ground when she sees Noh but there is nothing she can do. There is more to this slave, I believe, that no one else guesses. She will pass in our midst and my stares won't be noticed. Behind us, Mother and the elders wave goodbye beside the warriors who are left to guard the village. Mother, like a stone, tied to shore, watching the tribe come and go.

All that day, we travel along the shoreline. We do not stop. We pass cold deer jerky from hand to hand. Shilka sits in the bow of the lead canoe. He points to inlets, signposts that guide our way, naming each one. The shaman balances an obsidian bowl in his lap, cupping one hand over the top while fanning it with the other. Inside is a smoking rope carried from our winter fire-pit to start a new fire once we reach upriver. Without fire we will die. Only a person with power can carry the bowl.

As we steer, the fishermen tap a deerskin drum stretched over a hollow log. Drumbeats mark our movement. Drummers call out our pace. Drumbeats heat my veins in the damp spring air.

Salmon Beings, we are running toward you.
Salmon Beings, we are coming closer to you.
Salmon Beings, let me not fall asleep.
Let me not fall asleep
until I find you!

We canoe long into dusk, searching for a wide-mouthed river. We pass by stream after stream, but it is not the one.

"We will know it by the sign," says Shilka. "The

Ancient Ones painted salmon swimming on the rocks there. A special totem to call the fish to that river. Salmon have swam up it since we first came here from the Spirit World."

The sun is already setting that day when we spy rock cliffs hanging over the sea, painted black with salmon swimming upstream. We turn our canoes in the direction of our ancient fishing grounds. The river opens like a mouth leading into the dark forest.

Upward. To find them.

The river soon narrows and water rushes down toward us, flinging our canoes back. On each side, tall cedars stand guard over us. We step out to carry the canoes. Father lets the canoe sink down upon his shoulder. I walk behind him, the canoe riding high above my head. My father aims his body ahead, straight as an arrow. He alone must carry the burden of the whole tribe. If he can bring the fish back upriver, it will soothe First Uncle's spirit. The souls of the dead salmon will rest.

Upward.

Against this current, the fishermen tell me, salmon will soon struggle to swim. The mouth of this river is just the beginning of their long journey home. Some salmon will swim two or three moons to get upriver. They fight to reach the birthing grounds where they were born and where they will lay their eggs before they die. Heavy bodied, but so trim of tail that with one flick of it they can swim a warrior's length.

"We are here!" Father shouts at last.

I wonder, with evergreens hiding the moon and stars, how he knows where we are. I tumble into my red cedar bark mat upon the ground, trembling from the cold. I lay on my back and watch the sky. Somewhere in the distance, mountains tower, unseen. All around me, the fishermen rustle like dry leaves as they set up camp. I hear a roar in my ears like sea waves crashing. Perhaps it is the river's roar that deepens at night, like the sea.

I roll over to ask my sister if she hears it, but her head falls to the side, as if she fell asleep, listening. She smiles. Watching her, I no longer know who is my real sister—this one dreaming or the one I see at the Big House, scowling at her tasks.

I tell myself that I won't sleep just yet, that I will stay awake all night long. My mind is bright like a star. I will be the first to see what is around us come morning. Before anyone awakens, I will run down to the river. When the mists part, it will all rise up before me.

I shiver as the current roars down the mountains, with a chilly tingle of melted snow. I close my eyes and drift.

My last thought is, *This is where it all comes from.*

Where the
Salmon Leap

CHAPTER 8

Chinook Salmon Leaping

NANA

"Wake up!" Nanolatch nudges me. "The fishermen are gone."

The sky is blue-black. Only one star twinkles. Dawn. We race to the riverbank. The roar loudens. Water rushes over a high ledge of stone. I heard it all night and wondered what it was. Breath of the forest, I thought, but it is a cascading waterfall.

Something in me is swept away.

In the distance, mountains guard us, layers of them reaching higher and higher. Some are snow-capped. I have seen them all my life from the cliffs at sea. Now we squat in their shadow.

I have always paced by the sea, climbing the

cliffs for a better view. To see past the mists of that place. Water is my home. By the sea, women shut the world out as they weave. The night is longer than the day. Always gray.

Here, the skies are endless blue. Each leaf shimmers as if the world began in this place. The sunlight, even in early morning, warms my skin. A paradise. Fir and cedar reach high as the sky. I am all lit up, as if a thousand eulachon burned end to end inside me.

In a pool beneath the waterfall, the fishermen and taises bathe. Nanolatch and I stand shoulder to shoulder, watching them. He rubs his hands on his chest to show me how cold it must be.

"Men must cleanse all human scent to be pure enough to fish in the sacred fishing grounds," he shouts above the river's roar.

One by one, the fishermen shake themselves like dogs to dry off. My father walks over to us.

"Stay close to the river with the fishermen," he tells us. "Twins must wait for the salmon together. Each dawn. Each dusk."

My brother smiles at him. "There is no other place to be."

I can't help but watch the two of them together. My brother, aglow with my father's presence, stretching his neck to look up to him. My father always guides Nanolatch with words like treats you offer a pet. Father never speaks to me like that, never looks at me—only my brother. It is as if I do not exist.

Behind us Noh approaches with a load of water baskets for filling. She kneels on the bank beside us. But when my father notices her, he begins to shout.

"Go away!" He pushes her back from the river. "Come back in the afternoon."

"When the twins are together by the stream," Father explains to the fishermen, "that ghost must not go near them. She may be able to spin spells to harm the fish."

Noh scrambles into the woods. Nanolatch looks stunned, as if someone slapped him. He stares after the creature. But I hide my smile. There are places this slave cannot go that only my brother and I can.

By the afternoon, there is still no sign of fish. We set up the summer tents and racks that will be used to dry the salmon. The fishermen submerge a large cedar trap just below the waterfall. They say it will catch any fish that do not jump high enough. Mostly males will be taken. Females will be let free. Fishing will begin at dusk, the men promise.

That evening, we run down to the water. Dew drenches our feet. In the river, everything is moving. We stare until it is too dark to see clearly.

"Look there!" Second Uncle points to a whirling circle.

The fishermen creep to the edge. It is only a current trapped between two rocks. No sign of fish.

My brother and I huddle close for warmth.

"I wish the salmon would arrive," I whisper to

him. "The Chinook season is almost done. What if the sockeye don't run either?"

"Father says we must wait for them," he reminds me.

"They call us here in the cool morning, when we are half asleep, and again in the damp evening," I tell him. "But nothing happens."

"Those are the best times for fish to run, Nana. We must watch for them."

There must be another way for the salmon to run, I think, but I do not tell Nanolatch this. My brother does not question what our tribe does. But my mind swirls like a current, questioning everything I hear.

Early next morning Nanolatch and I hurry to the river while the fishermen still stretch out on their mats. We are so close to the water, it sprays our faces. The waterfall swallows our words. I close my eyes. It seems I am out at sea with the roar of wind and wave, where the Salmon Men live, growing and waiting for the day they will swim home.

Nanolatch taps my shoulder. Something blue flashes in the river like jewels. Water sprays our faces. We hear a great splashing from downstream. My stomach flips over as if a cold current rushes through me.

"It's a salmon run!" Nanolatch screams.

Bare feet pound the ground. Fishermen stand at our backs. At our feet swim huge salmon, shoulder to shoulder. They wiggle around boulders then spin on their tails. They leap above the waterfall, silver-bright in the morning light.

Father's eyes burn like the sun. He is the only one holding a spear. He spies the largest salmon waiting under the waterfall as if giving directions to the other fish. When the school leaps upstream, that salmon turns his head toward the waterfall and jumps. This is the moment Father awaits. He aims his spear and lets it fly. It slices through the back of the fish. It takes ten fishermen to splash in and lift the fish high, gleaming in their hands, wider and heavier than I am.

"Bless you, Salmon Twins!" The men cheer. "The Chinook salmon run for you!"

Nanolatch shrugs. "Father caught the fish. Thank him."

The fishermen laugh as if my brother has told a joke.

Father pats my brother's back. "It was you who called this salmon to the river. It is the blessing of the twins."

My brother's eyes darken with questions. I stand beside him but Father does not thank me.

"Find the shaman," orders Father. "We must begin the ceremony."

No one has to tell us where to find Shilka. He roams in the woods most days, collecting herbs and chanting to trees. They say he had a vision once of the sea rising and blood dripping off its edge. He opened his

mouth and drank all the blood, saving the sea from
foulness. Perhaps that is why we never get too close
to him. His breath reeks of rotting teeth. Around his
neck he has strung a charm of ten dead birds, decay-
ing. He can say and do whatever he wants. Everyone
obeys him, even my father.

"Salmon Twins, do you have something to tell
me?" His black eyes narrow.

Because he asks, I am free to answer. "Father
speared a salmon!"

"You bring good words," he croons. "Carry alder
wood to the shrine and kindle a fire so we can begin
the First Salmon ceremony."

After the flames die down, Shilka lays the
salmon on a flat stone. The tribe circles the fire-pit
where red embers glow.

"Swim upstream," the shaman chants.

Shilka paints the fish with red ochre and sprin-
kles it with sacred eagle down. He points its head
upstream so that all the salmon in the sea know in
which direction to travel home. He talks to it as if it
has a soul although it is dead.

I watch the smoke swallow the salmon in this
ceremony that honors his death and welcomes his
rebirth. He is called back from his death journey to
thank him for sharing his flesh. Soon he will drift
downstream, fleshless, a spirit without a body.

All afternoon the men pace. The sun hides
behind clouds. The shaman's voice darts in and out
of trees. No one eats. No one fishes. Herbs and

baked salmon smoke the air.

At dusk, Shilka drops the cooked salmon into our open palms. Crisp and sweet, we swallow it whole.

We know that only your bodies are dead here,
but your souls come to watch over us
when we are going to eat
what you have given us to eat now.

"We have sacrificed the First Salmon," Shilka says. "May his scent call the others."

The men rise with a shout. Grabbing spears, they rush to the river, Nanolatch and I at their heels. Salmon slip silvery through the dark water. Fishermen thrash in, thigh deep. Some lean out with nets to grab the fish as they jump. Arms stretch out to shoot arrows. The men shout and splash into the water, as if dancing with the salmon. Flashes of blue and silver dart across the evening air.

My brother's body tightens like a bowstring. His fists clench. He leans so far over the riverbank, I fear he will fall in. Next time, Father promises, he will toss his own harpoon. Soon he will swim away from childhood without me. He will join the world in which only men rule. Once we were whole, twin halves of the same Salmon Being. Now a crack opens between us, splitting us.

Just as the tears rise in my throat, something startles me. My mouth falls open. Above the men's voices, louder than the waterfall, I hear the soul of the First Salmon singing. He sings of sacrificing his flesh so we may live.

All night long I hear him chanting in the darkness to me. His voice rises to reach me as he journeys back down to the Salmon House by the sea.

There is no death, he sings, *only rebirth.*

The child I was, pieces of myself, swirl all around me. A million yearnings. A girl, secondborn, never enough. It gathers like a cloud above my head before it floats downstream with the Chinook.

CHAPTER 9

Step Between

NOH

He slips behind me like a cloak, his chants darkening the air.

Release my Spirit.
Give me the boy.
Let me enter into him.

All the other slaves stand apart from me, as if I were a lightning bolt that could strike them dead. Perhaps they sense First Uncle's ghost fly close by though none see him as I do. I have no choice but to listen, wishing I could swat him away like a mosquito, knowing I cannot.

Even from this distance, the wails of the salmon at sea beat like distant drums. Soon they will not brave the long journey upstream. Soon the girl's memory will return. I know these things in my bones.

By the river the boy watches. First Uncle finally drifts away from me to trail Nanolatch like a shadow. The boy paces, slamming the air with his fists. Something is building inside him, ready to burst. He keeps lookout as he is told, but he wants to do something. He knows that First Uncle would not stand still to mourn, wasting time. Something burns in Nanolatch—a longing to leap to manhood. But he has no harpoon, no magic herb. No secret way to transform himself. Everything churns inside him.

It hurts to watch this boy. It stirs all my sorrows like mud from a stream bottom. I pace in the woods, unseen, my footsteps matching his.

If I do this thing that First Uncle asks—if I can do it, if I allow it—this ghost will leave me. All the other ghosts haunting the burial grounds will go to sleep forever.

If I can do it.

Do I have this power that First Uncle believes I do? Flies on Wind had to stall the dead warriors so that I could talk to this ghost. Without her assistance, I never would have heard the uncle's wish. I always hoped to have such power after my Initiation. I have never acted alone before as a shaman, without a spirit guide. But how can I know I have this gift unless I try?

My mind roams back to my own village. Where did everyone go? If even one or two Salish were left wounded and still live, they will not be safe if these dead warriors burst out of the burial grounds, greedy for revenge. They will stir up killings, whisper evil up and down the coast against the Salish. Perhaps a child still roams there. If it's only one, let it be Dancing Bear, my brother, who hid so cleverly in our games that none could ever find him.

I must try to control these ghosts—even if I have never done such a thing before, even if I don't know how. Perhaps an animal helper will appear. The one I loved most since I was a child was the deer. Gentle and timid, it mostly hid, but always seemed to trail me secretly.

I will come close to the boy. First Uncle, always drifting at Nanolatch's side, will be watching and waiting.

I pray to the Spirits of my dead ancestors to allow me to do such a thing. I pray that the boy will not be hurt.

Not one drop of food or water will enter me. Until I do this deed, I will fast from the things of this world.

FEEDING THE RIVER

NANOLATCH

My heart pounds in the early morning run.
Beside the fishermen, with their spears held
high, I wait. The quick jerk of a net suspended
in mid-air. Arrows whizzing past. The long
wait at dusk. Silver tail fins beat a path
upstream. Blue backs splash through the river.
But the baskets fill slowly. Even the cedar
trap catches only a few salmon, unlike the
hundreds I was told were caught years ago. The
river is empty for days. When a hundred-pound
salmon runs by, he is untouched by any spear.
The men watch him with their breath held, as
if he has cast a spell.

I complain. "Why do you let this salmon pass
by?"

"Only the chief can kill such a large one for
the First Salmon Ceremony. If we let this one
pass, he will father many. A thousand fish will
run here in three years where once there was
only one."

Still the men murmur, counting their haul.
The day's catch lies upon the reeds. Too few
baskets are filled. Some of the Chinook have
turned color. As they near their spawning
grounds, the females become brown. Some

swim past us, already black. Such a fish is
never caught. Her flesh is bitter, without fat.
She bulges with eggs to be laid. We must let
her swim ahead.

"Heavy spring rain. Deep water. Snow melting in the mountains." Head Fisherman shakes
his head. "The Chinook should run stronger."

Shilka aims his staff straight in the fisherman's path. "The salmon have been disturbed.
Only a few Chinook venture out with spring. If
this continues, there will be less food each
year."

Father's face hardens like cliff stone. "Then
let us sacrifice. If we let twenty fish pass before
we aim for one, more will be able to spawn in
the sacred grounds this spring."

"It is a good plan," Shilka agrees. "The Chinook near the end of their run. We will wait
for the sockeye next."

"Next year the salmon will run strong
again," Father promises. "The Kwakiutl will do
what is right on the coast and the spirits will
reward us."

My arms hang heavily. This is my first time
here. Already the salmon are disappearing.
Some dare not leave the Salmon House. I never
got the chance to throw my own harpoon or
follow in First Uncle's footsteps. My father
may not be able to bring the salmon back, as
he hopes. I can't even look at him some days.

He grieves for the souls of the dead salmon.

The fishermen slumber. Day after day few fish
run. Shilka orders me to clean the salmon for
another ceremony. This is women's work, I
complain, but Father insists I do it. Nana
spreads the salmon flat, their white underbellies facing up. The fishwives teach me how to
slit them open with one knife stroke, then pull
the meat apart. I carve the red flesh while
Nana peels the skeleton free. I cannot talk
when I do this or look up, even if Raven Sun
calls me to play. I slice close to my sister's fingers and dare not look away.

Flesh falls from the bone. Long red strips to
dry on the racks. They will smoke over alder
wood fires and feed us all winter long.

When we are done, Shilka's bare feet stop in
front of me. When I look up, red ochre whiskers
are painted around his mouth. He stomps from
side to side, as if he just stepped out of the
water after a long swim. One who never
seemed man or woman is becoming a salmon.

"You must save every single bone," he gasps
for breath. "Do not spill one sliver on the
ground."

He jabs his staff at a trail of hair-like bones
so tiny we did not even notice them. Nana digs
on her hands and knees to scrape them up. Our
basket fills with bones. In the sun they gleam

like the pearly white insides of abalone shells.
Bones without flesh, they cling to the skeleton
as if the fish is still alive.

"Salmon Twins, lift the basket of bones.
Carry it to the river." Shilka hobbles ahead of
us, leading the way.

We lift the bone basket together. Behind
Shilka's back, I walk bowlegged to imitate him,
frowning. We must do as this shaman says,
even though I am the chief's son.

"Set it down here by the bank. Kneel beside
it."

In the distance Noh and the fishwives watch
like wooden statues. The wind blows. Shilka
towers above us, blocking the sun. We crouch
like two cold clams in his shadow.

"Throw the bones into the water."

As Shilka chants, we throw in the bones.
They float for a second before they twirl in circles of current and vanish downstream. There
is no trace of bone left anywhere. I remember
Second Uncle telling us how the Salish had
done what should never be done. They tossed
the bones of the salmon where the sun could
burn them.

Forbidden.

"Where do the bones go?" I question Shilka
after the ceremony.

"They float downstream to the Salmon
House."

"What do the salmon do with them?"

Shilka spins around, ten dead birds whirling around his neck. "Salmon are immortal! Their souls live in their bones. When you give the bones back to them, their souls weave their bodies back together. In deep, long winters beneath the sea, they grow red flesh around their bones."

Shilka drifts away, muttering chants to himself. Fishwives soon call my sister away to pick blueberries.

The shaman's words toss about in my mind. What is that force, I wonder, that changes these bones back into living beings? Transformation. Such magic—like the secret of becoming the bravest warrior—is what I crave. I pace by the riverbank so long the sun shifts in the sky.

I did not hear the slave come.

She has been ordered to stay away from us, but now that I am alone, she knows it is safe to do her work. Noh kneels in the stream beside me, filling a water basket. She leans far out, trapping the cleanest water. So still, apart from us all, in a world of her own. I do not think she even sees me.

Nearby, I hear thrashing in the bushes. A deer flies past, near the bank, startling the girl. Noh jumps up so quickly, her feet slip over the rocks. She screams, the first sound I have heard from her.

I do it without thinking. Grab her before she falls into the stream. Her body is as light as a willow branch in my hands. In front of me Noh squats, hiding her face like I am the chief. But I am the one who shakes. Something shoots through my body, from her into me, as if I have touched lightning with my bare hands.

"Stand up, Noh!" I order her.

She knows these words. Slowly she begins to unwind herself, cautiously, like a snake. She leans away, fearful of being kicked. We are almost eye to eye. So strange, the tiny tattoos dotting her cheeks, delicately carved. I wonder why she is marked that way. She must have been cut or burned to be marked so. The pain burning her, deep and slow. Did she cry out or wait, still within herself, as she does now? Did she bear it willingly or did she fight?

And then I see her black eyes shine as if wondering about me too. Her cheeks are round and full. Her plump lips fall open as if to speak. Her face seems just a mask she wears to cover herself.

I fill her spilled water basket. Together we walk back to the camp, side by side, sharing the weight of the basket between us. It must startle her to feel my hand beside hers, for her fingers tremble. She peeks at me from beneath a lock of wavy hair. I wonder what she sees.

My long, narrow nose? Or my chest, which I
pump full of air?

But then two fishermen pass by. I hear Noh's
sharp breath as she slows her step, pulling the
basket away. I pretend I do not notice how she
walks behind me, her head bowed. She changes
back into a slave.

"Don't get too near that one!" the fishermen
joke.

"Why?" I ask. "She's just a slave."

"See those marks on her face?" One points.
"Same as her mother. She's a shaman's daughter. Strange charms were found in her home."

I remember the villagers gasping when
Grandmother found the necklace of grizzly
bear claws around her neck. Sign of a shaman.
But the girl is too young, Shilka told us—not of
age to be initiated yet.

"What happened to their village?" I ask.

"Slashed to the ground, I hear. Not a totem
pole or person left standing."

I want to know more but I won't ask them.
Fishermen are full of gossip like their wives. If
I wish to know the truth, I must hear it from
the warriors who were there.

When I look up, the sun slants behind the
trees. Shadows deepen. Almost dusk. That's
when Nana appears, running to the river ahead
of me. It is easy to find my sister now. She
does not hide here. She either helps the fish-

wives or watches by the river.

"Salmon, let us find you," she churns the
water with both hands.

With each minute, the light dims. Soon
another day will end without any salmon.

"You must call too." Nana pokes me. "We
must do it together."

But before I can join her, her face suddenly
lights up like sun peeking through clouds. She
sees something—a quiver in the water, a flash
of red. The salmon's flesh touches hers. It
heard her voice calling from a far distance.
Everything whirls inside me. Ripping through
my belly. Burning.

From all the fishing tales I have heard, this is
the color I remember most. The crimson of
sunset spun with gold. Ripe salmonberries.
Flaming red.

"Sockeye run!" I scream.

I jump to my feet, waving to the fishermen to
come. Hoping the run will be enough. That
this time, the salmon will return forever.

But my sister gasps, her mouth fallen open.
She stares at me as if I have given away all her
secrets. The salmon run just for her, swimming
into her hands, and I have told everyone.

Too late.

Feet slam down. Fish leap. Harpoons and
spears fly through the air. One in twenty is
theirs. My heart leaps with them, a heart that

had been pierced with First Uncle's fall. This is where his stories came from. His aim steady. Jumping higher than anyone. He was on his way home to teach me these things.

I splash into the ice-cold river. With my bare hands, I lift a fallen salmon high. They can't tell me to wait. I won't anymore. I won't be still. I won't listen. My time is now. I will be the fisherman First Uncle was.

He is here.

Chanting the Salmon songs. Whispering the secrets of catching them. Flashing his harpoon before me. He dips down from The Country of the Ghosts to teach me. I dance in the sunlight, where the silvery sparks fly.

His soul swims in the water beside me.

CHAPTER 10

Blackberry Summer

NANA

Too soon it is midsummer.

A word that means something far away, eternal, a word sounding like the hot breath of summer drops down like a rockslide. I have spent the summer days chasing Nanolatch, cleaning salmon from the bone, running in the shade-cool woods and never stopping to think since we first set up camp.

Suddenly, with a word, it is over. Midsummer.

I should have known it when the blackberries ripened. But it is my first summer here and I did not yet know, as the fishwives did—those who picked beside me. Blackberries spill their sweetness into the last of summer's days.

Already shadows spread deeper. The sun rises later and sets earlier. A chill lifts from the earth at dusk. Nights, we huddle in our mats.

One morning I awaken to find Father pacing. My mother once said that you have only to look at a chief to understand his tribe. His flesh tells a story. His bare skin is burnt reddish-brown from working in the sun. His chest is wide from years of paddling on the open sea. He has brought years of plenty to our tribe—bountiful fish and game—until this summer.

But my father's words shake the earth. "We leave today."

His words bang like drumbeats against my chest. An order to be obeyed. His voice always final.

I run to find Nanolatch and drag him back. Father will listen to him. All the fishermen buzz about my brother's speed in the water. He spent hours chasing the fallen fish for them. First Uncle's spirit enters him, they whisper. He is the chosen one. Second Uncle frowns to hear it.

"Please, Father!" I beg with my brother beside me. "We want to stay longer."

Immediately he shakes his head. "The elders have been alone too long. The warriors who guard them will worry if we do not return."

"There is so much to do here!" My brother tugs his arm. "We have not yet swam in the pool beneath the waterfall. And we have not climbed to the mountaintop."

"Next year, there will be time," he pats Nanolatch's head.

"Next year is far away!" I blurt out.

I burn with a fire to stay. Not just another day, as my brother wants. That would not be enough. I want to live here forever.

Father crosses his arms over his chest. "Walk to the river with me and I'll show you why we must go."

It is early morning, the best time for fishing. But no fishermen are around. Father points upstream. Falling down from the waterfall are tiny fish, the size of a finger, silvery, with transparent red bellies.

"The old salmon have died," he explains. "The young that hatched a year ago are leaving the breeding grounds. These smolts begin to head back to sea in midsummer and so must we."

Father glances downstream, thinking of our journey, and of the elders who await us there, their food stores dwindling. The fishermen arrive, without spears, awaiting orders.

"You may swim in the pool this morning." He turns away to greet the men. "We leave later today."

I glare at my brother. "Father forgets we call the salmon. Let's call them back and show him we must stay."

Nanolatch watches the men load the canoes. I bend down and run my hands through the sun-touched river. One of the smolts smacks his tail against the water, slamming it hard. He tilts his head to watch us with one eye. Then he darts off, chasing the other fish. He nudges each one with his fin, leading them downstream.

"There is nothing we can do to make the salmon stay," Nanolatch sighs.

I look up at the mountains. They lean over as if they could touch me. Leaving brings a stab of pain to my chest. I feel as if I am struggling deep underwater, unable to breathe.

Upstream, the pool gleams in the sun.

Nanolatch springs up. "Let's swim, Nana. We can splash as much as we want."

All that morning we swim and splash in the water. The pool reaches up to my neck, sun-warmed on top, chilled on the bottom. We jump straight into the waterfall, pretending we are salmon, tumbling back down into the pool, tossed by the current. The fishermen's laughter ripples like waves on the air as they watch.

By the time we come out, the camp is down and so are the drying racks. Chinook and sockeye fill thirty baskets. Not enough to last the winter. The men talk on and on, my brother hanging on every word as if they were sweet berries. No one notices when I slip away and head back to the riverbank for one last goodbye to the salmon.

What can I do there but chant the songs that only the salmon from this river know, songs Grandmother sang to me when I was little? Lines you cannot write down or tell anyone. My words hum underwater, vibrate from stone to stone, echo down the river, and ripple along the coast. Into my open hands, the smolts soon wiggle. This river is a language that runs deep in their cold veins.

I tell no one that, beneath my hands, the young salmon swarm.

I do not know how long I squat there before I sense the bushes parting. Someone is near. I spin around. Noh stands behind me, stiff as a totem pole. She stares without blinking at the fish. No one must know I call them on my own. My brother already betrayed me, calling the fishermen.

I keep still and wait. That is what Grandmother always teaches me to do. Noh does not run to call the tribe. She does not move. A thought flashes through me. *She knows what I am doing and keeps it quiet.* Then a shiver blows through me, chilling me. I thought Noh was one of the Spiritless Ones. For the first time, I sense her thinking. Like a sea sponge, she fills herself with the knowledge of what I am doing and holds it within.

I stare at Noh. I never really noticed her before. She stands tall, her hair wavy and wet as if she bathed herself just as we do. Her eyes widen as I turn and her breath catches in her throat.

Then I remember. *Do not kill the innocents.* She is one of them.

Men's voices shout behind us. I churn up the waters to scare the fish away. Then I lean over to yank a stone from the muddy underbelly of the river. I stuff it into my pocket.

"I'll be back," I whisper to the river.

The fishermen float the canoes in the river and we head downstream.

"You have chosen the best of all days for our trip," the men yell to my father. "The current runs swift. The water is still high. And the wind blows at our backs."

Our canoes press against rock like a drawn bow-string. In the currents, the young fish swim past. Pulled toward the Salmon House. Pushed by wind. Called by sea. We fall downhill, down toward the sea.

For a full day, we journey.

Ahead is the blue rise of the sea, the red cliffs by the shore, and smoke drifting out of the plankhouses. My grandmother waves from the sand. All the elders surround our canoes when we land, counting the summer's catch.

The welcome look in their eyes fades.

"Next year," Father promises them, "there will be more fish."

The elders murmur, holding tight to one another's arms. They stand in a circle long after dusk, staring out to sea.

I look out with them. The sea is a giant mouth that will swallow me. It is where I will be tied to shore, so that I cannot wander far. My hiding place known. My work measured. The Way chosen.

My heart is heavy as stone. I will live by the sea

for another year far from home. Far from the riverbanks. Far from what I have begun to know in my bones.

THERE ARE NO ACCIDENTS

NOH

To step between the living and the Dead is to be set on fire from skin down to bone. Straight to the ground I dropped. Everything sizzled inside when the ghost shot through me. All I wanted was to drench my body in that cold stream.

Nanolatch lifted me up so delicately, as if I would break. His touch was sunlight. He may clutch a weapon and look like his uncle the warrior, but inside his heart is gentle. His hands spoke another language. I flushed, quickly lowering my head so he would not see. In the woods the deer's hooves pounded as he ran off from his task.

I stood close to the boy for the first time. He with his smooth, bare chest and the deepest, darkest eyes I have ever seen. His eyelashes, each one, thick and curled. His hair, sleek and shiny like a seal's coat.

He watched me too, studying my tattoos and the necklace that has frightened the tribe. I

don't remember how it came to me for it was
my mother's. Perhaps he finds me ugly com-
pared to the Kwakiutl girls, tiny and swift at
their chores. But he bends to help me fill my
water basket without a word.

How it stung to hear the fishermen warn him
against me. But even worse is the tale they told
of my village where no one lives. No one left
to bury the Dead. I understood their every
word. But I pretend that I am dumb, maybe
even deaf. Let them think I move in a dreamspell. To them, I must be invisible.

I keep trying to return to my village in the
only way I know how—my dreams. But nothing is there except the ghosts and thick, white
fog I cannot see through. The Salish all lay
slain on the sand as they were when I left. All I
wish is to bury them so that their Spirits will
find rest in The Country of the Ghosts. It is
taboo not to bury your dead. This is the Kwakiutl's revenge for the bones.

The Salish did not know what our fishermen
in those five canoes did. They were young
men, newly initiated, full of boasts. They
chose to fish on their own with no elder. We
marveled at their great catch. One day, their
canoes were loaded with the biggest salmon we
had ever seen. Father questioned them, for it
was not the season for such fish. Their eyes
darted. Quick-tongued, they lied. Snakes in our

midst. Wind Tamer advised the Salish to visit
the Salmon House to make amends, to drop
the bones down and offer prayers. We were set
to leave the following day. But the Kwakiutl
war canoes stormed in first. The innocent fell
with the guilty.

I would go back if I could, but they watch me
closely. Besides, the way is long by foot. Only a
guardian spirit would know the path to take. I
await the dream when Wind Tamer will call
me to bury her. But no such dream has come.

First Uncle has left me. He lingers like a dim
glow around Nanolatch. All the fishermen feel
it. I pray the ghost will be true to his word that
his warriors will not ever roam in the land of
the living.

The brother and sister have both noticed me
now. They look into my eyes unlike the rest of
the tribe, who step back. To these two and
their grandmother, I am not invisible.

The boy will grow in power now, filled with
his uncle's strength. But the girl is trapped. No
spirit helper has found either her or me.

She is one who speaks to the salmon. She is a
mystery, like the salmon who find the way
back to their childhood home, running up the
same river that pushed them down to sea.
Pulled by stars. Swept by wind. Such yearning
they both have.

I have heard that salmon sometimes travel

unknown streams and lose their way, die without spawning far from home. A picture forms in my mind—Nana on the cliffs, looking out for the one who is missing.

She is just like them.

There are no accidents in this life, my mother taught me. Everything fulfills the Way— pain, death, love. All are spread out on the same path. We must follow it to find our way, whatever it brings.

It has brought me to the twins.

Place of Mists

CHAPTER 11

Transformation Potlatch

NANOLATCH

Darkness fell like a surprise that autumn. Quick and black after the dazzling sun upriver. One afternoon, Nana and I roamed across the sand at low tide, collecting shells. But my sister soon disappeared, scrambling up on the rocks that push out from the bay. Far out she climbed to the boulders towering over the sea, where the water is deep and cold.

Our mother paced the shore, shouting her name. *"Nana! Nana! Get back here!"* I heard that name spill in the damp air. Mother studied the spot where my sister climbed. But my sister surfaced in another spot far off, where you would not think to look for her. Dangerously close to the waves, she hung over the rocks.

"Get ready!" When Father appeared with that shout, we both ran to the beach, to ready ourselves. Sweet smells had drifted from the fires for days. Whistles shivered from the woods that dawn, announcing a potlatch. Finally when darkness fell, we saw the Nootkas' canoes dart by, ten seagoing canoes in a row with a hundred taises dressed in red ceremonial robes.

I rush into the Winter Ceremonial House and settle beside my sister. She no longer looks twelve. Her hair is loose, unbraided, and sleek with seal oil. Her robe falls to her ankles. Around its hem, rows of dog salmon twirl. My mother says that, year by year, girls change. Whatever lives deep in their bones, shadows of our ancestors, drifts upward. In my sister's face tonight, I see my mother's full cheeks and Grandmother's narrow eyes full of secrets. Something else too—a drawing back, as if she isn't here. She yearns to be someplace else.

We face the tall totem poles carved by our great-great-grandfather. Dangling from hidden strings above our heads, small wooden Salmon totems spin in the air. They are as big as a man's hand, left behind by our great-great-grandfather, staring at us with abalone eyes.

Everything is moving.

Around the fire in the middle of the house, the Nootkas and Kwakiutls are seated. Shadows touch the ceiling. Smoke from candlefish burning end to end clouds the air, choking me. Piles of treasures are everywhere. Gleaming coppers. Elk hides. Sea otter skins. Cedar bark blankets. Newly carved cedar canoes in a row by the door. My mother's woven dog-hair blankets spun of yellows and blacks and reds.

Father claps his hands. One by one, my mother and aunts carry these treasures to each Nootka taise—our guests. The coppers now belong to the Nootka chief and his young son. My mother's blankets are placed in the hands of the chief's wife. How their faces glow in the firelight as they receive their gifts. The coppers burn with their own leaping fire. The Nootkas are honored. Father beams, sitting tall. Each and every guest has a gift, sign of our wealth. No one guesses that our wealth dwindles with the disappearing salmon.

The women of my family carry in food. Trays pass from hand to hand. Deer. Bear. Roasted duck. Seal. All our dried salmon. Spruce leaf tea. Wild beach peas. Currants. Hot clams slide into my mouth. Ten fish skeletons are all that remain on my plate. We must fill our bellies full until they ache. It is expected at potlatch. I toss my head back and laugh, for Nana always teases me that I eat each night like I am at potlatch. Thick smoke fogs the air like clouds. We all await the dance next.

Shilka circles the fire in a cedar skirt.

"Tonight, you will see transformation. Only the

purest warrior and maiden will succeed the trials of
Initiation that await young Kwakiutls."
I lean forward. Beside me my sister sits rigid as a
cedar tree. She tosses a flat stone from palm to
palm, eyeing the doorway. She listens to something
afar—not in this room, not of this moment.
Elders beat on deerskin drums and hollow logs.
Flames leap high when eulachon oil is flung into the
fire. A boy crawls past us. Behind him a tall dancer
appears, wearing a cedar raven mask with a long
pointed beak. The boy warms himself by the fire.
The raven figure dances with his arms outspread,
swooping close. It taps its wooden beak together.
Still the boy does not turn. We hold our breath.
Slowly the beak creaks open, yanked by hidden
strings.
Deep inside is what all who live by the sea fear.
A thousand tales of Sisiutl's power have we heard.
He is the sea monster from the bottom of the sea, a
serpent with two heads whose evil kills souls.
The boy rises up slowly as if being pulled. Six
green eyes fix upon him. Tongues spit like fire.
Sisiutl looks with serpent eyes through the young
boy. The boy falls down.
A blanket covers the fire. All is black. Everyone
gasps. When the light returns, the boy vanishes.
Another boy is shoved into the circle. He sees
Sisiutl at once. The boy runs, the clamshells tied to
his ankles chattering. But he turns his head back.
Few can look upon Sisiutl and remain standing.

Something hisses like a snake. The sea creature's tongue juts out and his green eyes roll. Sisiutl taps the boy with his beak. The boy's face becomes stone. He roams around the room, passing by Noh and the slaves who crouch in the doorway. The young boy becomes one of the Spiritless Ones.

A man with a copper shield jumps out from a wooden chest. Sisiutl whirls around. He spits and clucks, stamping his claw feet. The man twirls a weapon of cedar and bone. First Uncle's harpoon! The sea monster looks up at it, dazzled. Swiftly the man plunges the harpoon into Sisiutl's chest. The creature falls down. We all cheer.

A hundred eulachon are heaped onto the fire. It blazes like a bonfire. Shilka passes First Uncle's harpoon through the flames, smoking hot, then straight into my open hands.

"This is your weapon to face the trials of Initiation."

I glow like the moon. Uncle's Spirit returned to me at the waterfall and now his harpoon, too. With it, I can transform myself.

Darkness suddenly falls.

In the dimness, a young girl wrapped in bark and goat hair is trapped in a cage. She must be on her fasting trial. Warriors dressed as trees stand by. I nudge Nana but she does not turn. The girl crouches, unable to move. Her eyes dart in her face, flashing in the darkness. Trees sway. Animals cry. The moon rises and falls. Many days pass. Evil spirits call out. And then a huge creature with an owl mask rushes into the circle. He rips the twig cage apart. The girl screams. The owl reaches in to grab her.

"Ugh! Ugh!" a deep voice grunts.

The Ceremonial House shakes. Everyone turns, even the owl. A giant woman stomps into the room. She has stringy hair and long breasts, and she wears a black mask. She snatches a child and tosses it into her sack. All the children crawl into their mother's laps and bury their heads.

"Dzonokwa!" Grandmother whispers to us.

"Kidnapper!" scream the mothers.

Dzonokwa stares with hollow eyes and a wide, empty mouth. She creeps closer and closer to the young girl. Her cedar skirt rustles.

The trees stomp with a thump like heartbeats. They chant,

Here comes Dzonokwa
who carries off humans in her arms,
who makes us faint.
Great bringer of nightmares!

All around us, villagers shiver. I stretch to get a glimpse of Noh. In the doorway, she crouches, so pale, staring without blinking at the creature. The owl does not move. Dzonokwa blows like a windstorm. The girl stumbles over to the creature. Dzonokwa then kicks the owl until it rolls over, dying, and hands the girl the two salmon totems.

The girl bows before Dzonokwa, begging her to release the small child. When the child runs free, we all cheer.

Darkness.

When the fire blazes again, Shilka passes the totems through the flames. He gives them to my sister.

"The answers you seek are within."

In my sister's hands the totems gleam. One of the totems lifts her arms to dive. Her arms are frozen forever upward as she holds the Chinook salmon high. The other totem is tall and trim, a harpoon at his side. Nana squeezes them both tightly while Grandmother looks on, smiling.

Drumbeats roll. Shilka raises his staff and stamps it down.

"Salmon Twins, never stand by the river alone or travel there without the tribe. You are of the spirits, and we must keep you safe."

Suddenly Shilka flinches as if something flies in the air above him. He crouches low down. Everyone grows hushed. The shaman's body clenches, stiff as a totem. His eyes roll back into his head.

Another voice, not his, speaks out of his mouth. A voice without a body. Deep and clear.

"You both are born from the Chinook salmon. Each of you has a special destiny."

Father dares to ask, "What is his destiny?"

Shilka's mouth twists. "To save the tribe. One to rule on land. One on the sea. That is all we can say."

Father and Second Uncle both stare at me. In that very moment my chest lifts as if I have grown as tall as Father. I will begin my trial with the harpoon of our finest fisherman. I will rule after my father. I am the only son.

We all hear Shilka hiss the chant next. Like some evil spirit, words puff from his mouth in rings of smoke.

One to rule on land.
One to rule on sea.
Shall it be you or me?

The shaman shakes himself, swinging his long hair. He stands up and looks around the Ceremonial House.

The trance is broken. Everyone claps at the performance. My sister's brown eyes search mine. I turn away from her. It is deep, deep dark.

Afterward I lie down with the harpoon at my side. My mind drifts in the smoke. My belly is stuffed. Before I shut my eyes, my sister disappears like she always does. She does not stay with our young cousins who call after her, piled up one on top of the other. Sleep soon rides over me like waves.

But in the middle of the night, eerie cries awake me. Half bird. Half cougar. Something has been let loose, some evil that has been buried deep. Surely it is not a human cry. It is a long while before I close my eyes again.

CHAPTER 12

Memory Returning

NANA

Cries from the beach—sharp as fir needles digging
into my flesh—call me. I must go. I step outside the
Ceremonial House where everyone sleeps after the
first long night of potlatch.

All except Noh.

By the shoreline, ravens gather as she dances.
They circle high above her head with sharp caws.
Below them she spins. My footsteps stop on the
sand. Noh tosses stones up to the ravens. The stones
steam like fog in the cold night air. When the stones
fall back down into them, her hands must sizzle for
she waves her arms wildly. Not one sound do I hear
from her lips, only the maddening caws of the birds.

I step closer. But the moment my foot lifts, Noh vanishes into smoke.

Why has she come here before me? I wonder. Perhaps she senses what I want—to know my Way. Deeply I sigh. Everyone knows their Way except me. Never would I want to go on an Initiation trial alone in the deep woods to meet any of the evil spirits who live there.

I belong near water, always.

One to rule on land. One to rule on sea.

The voice that spoke through Shilka sets a cliff between my brother and me, defining us. Between the two of us there has never been distance. We thought we were the same. We never turned toward the future. Now he will step toward it without me. But why can't I help him?

I creep along the rocks, farther and farther out. In my hands, I still clutch the river stone. Since I left upriver, I have carried it everywhere. I want to swim out and touch the tip of the world, with no distance between the sea and me. I want to be part of it. Glide like a fish. Swirl with the underwater creatures. Transform myself into another being.

No one is here to stop me, not even my mother. Down from the cliffs, away from the rocks, she always calls me. Out of the water, she would pull me too. Her voice forever spills my name on the humid air.

Nana! Stay home! Be like me! Stay safe!

I know what I must do then. I shed my garment

and drop into the sea. Its salty arms slip around my neck. I am never allowed to do this when my mother watches. Immediately, my body stiffens with the shock of the cold water.

If only I could go out far enough to where the Salmon House is. There the young Salmon Men wait for next spring when they will brave the river again. If only I could swim close enough for them to hear me.

"Swim home in spring," I call to them. "I will be waiting upstream."

I fling the river stone far as I can. It arches high and then sinks down. I want it to reach deep into the Salmon House beneath the sea. But it is a day's long canoe ride away.

And then the memory comes.

I was there once.

A dark place opens wide, a space before thought or words. I must have been to a ceremony at the sacred fishing grounds. That's why it seemed like home upriver. My brother does not remember it or he would have told me.

Warriors had carried us, their bone-tipped spears glinting like sun on sea water. I lay in their hands, newborn red. Above me floated the universe. The sky. The eagle's slow circles around the mountaintop. Beneath me rushed the river, cool and deep. The spirits poured their blessings over me there. But what the spirits said, what promises they stamped upon the two of us, I do not remember.

Suddenly I feel my body trembling. My arms quiver. Beside me, the rocks are close by, but I can't reach out to them. My heart races. I can't catch my breath. Even my muscles betray me, cramping into a tight ball. I wished to become a sea creature, but I have no strength to swim. The beach closes like a shell, beyond my reach.

Soft air blows upon me a sweet, intoxicating breath. I hear a voice in my ears: *Be calm. Turn toward shore. Exhale deep. Inhale deeper.* I am lifted.

Back on the rocks, I flop down, breathless. My chest heaves like a snared fish. Onto the hard surface, my body sinks. I drift somewhere that is neither awake nor asleep. A place where there is no thought. By the time I get up, the moon is descending. A blanket wraps me tight. I tiptoe inside the Ceremonial House where everyone is dreaming. Close to the fire, beside my cousins, I curl up, still shivering. There is no room at Nanolatch's side in my old spot. First Uncle's harpoon takes my place.

Noh, the one who has been my constant shadow, awaits me. She is not sleeping. Her hair streams out around her, shiny as if wet. A few moons ago, my face flamed with shame if she followed me. But now, as she lies down by my mat, holding our dog Yamunah, I stretch out and drift. Noh's dark eyes study me like some guardian spirit. And then I sleep. The dreamworld closes its arms around me, pulling me out where I cannot go in this world— with this body.

GIRLS FROM ANOTHER WORLD

NANOLATCH

Sisters can drift. They can daydream. All they
have to do is look beautiful like my mother,
who endlessly braids her hair, awaiting my
father. Nana could just sit still and listen to
Grandmother's stories forever. Drift in a
dreamspell by Shilka's side throughout the
long winters. Fill her head with dancing spirits.
These worlds exist, as they say, but my way is
with the living, not the Dead.

I feel a hundred years older than Nana. With
her games and hideaways, she is still a child.
Always tugging at me. As if I could go with her
anytime I please. Shrug off this cloak of dread
I wear. Blood of the past. Fear of revenge.
Starvation our future by the time I become
chief. My Way is hauling fish in, each day
becoming stronger. It is what the tribe expects
of me.

Already there are narrow-eyed stares from
the elders when I return home from a day at
sea. Weighing my catch. Studying the fishermen's faces to judge if I have done well, if I
am my father's son. Counting the days I near
Initiation. They all hang on me.

With uncle's harpoon I catch prize halibut

now, guessing where they hide, striking them as they swim past. Surely that is being the ruler of water. On land I do more than my share. I rush to be first to follow Father's orders to pull the canoes in at dusk, to unload our catch, to cart fallen trees from the forest for our fire. Surely the salmon totem is so strong within me that I will be given power to avenge—a warrior's right.

There is only one thing I am not quite sure of. I have no power to understand any girl. Girls seem to have dropped down here from another world and never quite touch the sand. Before Noh came, I never bothered looking deeper. Now I wonder all the time.

One afternoon, Noh walked with two water baskets out from the path that led to the springs. Dripping wet, the slave's hair shone reddish black in the sunlight. Just her face was uncleansed. Thick lines of wood ash streaked her cheeks, a sign of mourning. Though she had been with us for many moons, she seemed to have awoken just then to realize she had lost everyone.

I wanted to reach out and help her carry a basket, as I did once before. But it was daylight, and once we stepped onto the beach, everyone would have seen us together. Taboo for a chief's son to even look at a slave. I stopped in my tracks.

But I cannot forget her touch at the riverbank
and how, ever since, I no longer mourn First
Uncle. Inch by inch, I am becoming him. Can
one touch from this shaman girl heal me?

I can't help staring at her. I wonder what
makes Noh different. I think it is her eyes,
how they look through me whenever she is
near. She reads the secrets hidden in my heart,
as if she could see inside me. I admire the way
she walks when she goes about her chores. So
smooth and curved, she glides like a fish
through waves.

Yet she changes in an instant when the men
are near. If my father enters the plankhouse,
Noh presses against the wall like a shadow, her
eyes darting between him and the fire, waiting
for one to speak and the other to ebb. When
the fire dies down, she rushes for wood to feed
it. Sometimes, when my father snaps his fingers, Noh suddenly jerks as if she had fallen
asleep, dreaming, sitting straight up. She
flinches when he calls, and rushes to his side.

All I know about Noh is that she was a
shaman's daughter, and that her spirit drifts,
somewhere far from here, perhaps in Salish
land. I wait until Second Uncle and I are seated
alone one night. He has been telling me stories
of all the raids he has been on since his
Initiation. Father would never tell me such
things.

"Fifty men fell within minutes of our landing. We conquered that village, loaded up our canoes with furs and blankets, and were back home by the next day. Not one scratch did I receive. That was my first raid."

"Weren't you afraid?" I wonder.

"Of the warriors in that village?" He tosses his head back and laughs. "They were nothing. Dogs. Not human. I am of the Raven Clan, descended from the gods."

Second Uncle spends his days with his face still blackened, dipping often into an icy stream to bathe, and wears his hair in a bundle on top his head, ready for battle. He refuses to speak to most of the villagers, only the taises. He will not even eat with us. About the village he stalks, glaring at everyone as if the enemy is nearby.

My teeth clench, listening to him. First Uncle never spoke that way. He loved the sea, boasting of his catch of fish, not men. Not one detail of the raids did he share. His heart was not in them. Your heart must be gone to be a warrior. Killing, the one thing on your mind.

"What happened during the last raid on the Salish coast?" I ask.

"The Salish were prepared. Some came running with spears when we landed—though not the leader, who wanted to talk. Our men fell fast. That made me kill harder and faster. I cut their leader down in the middle of his sentence."

I suck in my breath. "The fishermen say the entire village was destroyed. But they did not say what happened to the women and children. Just one slave was captured and brought home—Noh. Why not more?"

Second Uncle narrows his eyes. He looks around to see if anyone nearby is listening. He leans close.

"When my brother went down, your father called a halt to the killing. By that time, most of the Salish men were on the ground, dying. The women had fled with their children up to the woods, except for that ghost girl. Our chief ordered us not to chase them. We left them unharmed."

I clear my throat so he will not hear me gasp. "Why did Father do this?"

"He sorrowed for our brother. Warriors should not have a heart. I say we should have slaughtered every last one of them. For, like snakes, they will gather someday and rise up against us in revenge."

I wonder if Noh guesses any of this. In my mind, I see her so clearly, as if she were stamped there. Anointing of ash upon her face. Head bowed. How she drifts, half ghost, floating through our village. I do not think she knows any of her tribe still lives. If she believed this to be so, she would be alert. Her eyes would shift like a sly dog, seeking a way to escape. I vow to my uncle I will tell no one. Noh would be the only one who wished to hear it anyway.

My mind is swirling. To be a warrior is to slaughter someone like Noh.

CALLING CEREMONY

NOH

Outside the village, the spirits of the fifteen warriors lay still on their planks in the burial grounds. Gray as fog. See-through. Piece by piece, they begin their journey to The Country of the Ghosts. Let them sleep on.

Not one bite of the potlatch feast did I touch.

Out to the beach I crept, with the hot stones I secretly stole from the potlatch fire hidden in my basket. In the dark, I twirled until I was dizzy, making my head spin. From palm to palm, I tossed the hot stones. They burned my flesh so I called out to the spirits. The ravens arrived, beating the air above my head with their flat, black wings, cooling the sting. They flew in circles, fiercely croaking. Somewhere this happened before—ravens clustering above me, announcing.

My body was a shell I left on the sand. My mind cleared. I called to the spirits to allow me to help the girl. Her destiny is with the salmon but she does not remember what it is. I watched when the twin totems were placed in her hands, like sparks to awaken the fire that sleeps within her. Someone must yank her from her dreams.

I called and called her out, spinning in my dance until the potlatch was done. And still I spun. Then she walked out to the beach in her white garment. I knew what I must do. Bring her out there, into the sea from which she came, out to the Salmon House. I wished to send her a vision, a memory.

I spun myself into a wisp of fog. She no longer saw me crouching behind a totem pole. Into the waters she dropped, spreading her arms wide to embrace the waves. From my hiding spot, I felt the memory dip down into her.

But she stayed in the water too long. The sea began to claim her. I stretched out from the rocks and grabbed her. Blew a spell upon her, calming her, so she would not remember my coming. I pulled her onto the rocks, waiting for her breath to return.

I should not have called her out there. She was not strong enough. I forgot that she is more human than spirit.

If I could let her see the Salmon House just
once, if she could get near, it will change her.
She will be punished, but she will live through
it. It would strengthen her like a meal of
steaming deer heart.

The longing must brand her soul. It must
grow like appetite.

CHAPTER 13

Spinning the Day

NANA

The sea is an endless rush and roar, a voice without a body. If I am still and listen closely, Grandmother promises, I shall hear the Salmon Men growing. But I must not think. I must hold steady, my breath and the ocean's breath one, so that I cannot tell one from the other. I will not know where I end and it begins.

I have seen my brother a mile out, his harpoon shooting in the air like a Chinook salmon leaping. At dawn he jumps when the men call him. He passes by, his eyes straight ahead. My brother dives into his work like a fish into sea. I wonder where he is—the brother who spoke my thoughts aloud.

He is everywhere but here.

At dusk Nanolatch lingers on the beach. He collects stones that roll in, bits of granite and quartz, washed smooth by waves.

"Do you want to climb the cliffs?" I run up to him.

Silence. Nanolatch picks up a chip of abalone. It gleams like a treasure.

"You never have time for me anymore," I tell him.

He snaps back. "I have work to do. There is no time to play."

His words sting like wasps.

"But we don't do any of the things we used to do!" I complain.

I study his face, leaner and darker than mine. No longer the boy who came when I called.

"I have more important places to go," he boasts. "Tomorrow Father will take me out to the Country Beyond the Ocean!"

My heart beats in my mouth. The men will travel somewhere I yearn to see. Secretly. Without me.

"Can I go?" I beg.

Nanolatch turns away. Useless to ask such a thing.

That evening I whisper to Noh to awaken me in the middle of the night, when the fire loses its red-hot glow. She sits up, watching the fire, her face ash-streaked. Not one word does she say. When she shakes me hours later, I jump up. It is still dark. The half-moon crooked in the sky. One last star close by, keeping it company. We rush to the fishing canoes. In the largest one—my father's—I set a tall fishing basket in the stern.

"There will be no time to fish," I tell her. "It's a long journey where they are going."

I squirm into the basket and tell Noh to cover me with seaweed. Her eyes study me darkly. Then she hides me, wedging the lid on tight, closing me in.

Before dawn I hear them coming. Father barking orders. Nanolatch shouting with excitement. A few fishermen talking.

"We will ride hard without stopping, each of us taking turns," Father tells them. "It is far and we must return by dark."

The men push out to sea. The only sound is the endless splash of paddles through water. Later the sun beats down on my basket. Mid-day. Inside, it is hot and hard to breathe. Finally, as the fishermen race the canoe, Father and Nanolatch both huddle down out of the wind. I hear them murmur.

"One of my children will rule the land and sea someday," my father says. "Before I pass them on to you, I must do what I can to bring the balance back."

"You have done enough," my brother tells him. "Warred. Defended the salmon. You even took less at the fishing grounds."

Father is silent. Our canoe bumps from side to side, making my belly heave.

"I have failed, son. I sacrificed everything, even my own brother. War brought us more sorrow. That is why I wish to visit the Salmon House. Listen to their song. Hear what they ask. Know if they forgive us."

Nanolatch raises his voice. "But the Salish also did a terrible thing!"

"We are all responsible. Each of us must obey the Way. You have always done so. But, see, over there—we come to it!"

The paddles stop. The canoe slows. Around me, the fishermen gasp.

"Look!" someone yells.

Father chants the ancient songs to the dead souls of the salmon. They are the songs he learned from Grandmother as a young boy—the songs she teaches me now. All the men are silent.

I uncoil myself like a snake, and inch upward. Prying the top of the basket a crack, I peek out. In front of me the men stand, staring straight ahead. It is a marvelous place of sun and sea—sunbeams of such brightness, it stings my eyes. No land in any direction. Water churns in an endless circle. It spins like a vortex, hypnotizing us. I feel like diving into it. It seems like the center of the world.

Just then, a fisherman turns, and I drop back down into the basket.

"Listen!" someone calls. "They are answering now."

"What are they saying, Father?" my brother asks.

Their wails sound like something pierced in half. It makes my whole body writhe. The cry lifts higher and higher on the wind.

My father sighs. "They still mourn...nothing has changed."

His voice is hollow, just an echo. "They demand sacrifice. I cannot give it to them. But there will be no end to their loss unless we do."

"What can we sacrifice?" my brother asks.

Again the long silence. Then my father cries out, beating on the cedar side of the canoe, shaking me.

"No! No! I won't allow it! I will meditate instead. Let us go from here. Head home!"

The canoe flies off. My brother calls my father's name over and over. But there is no answer. How I wish to be the one beside him. It isn't your fault, I would say. But I can't say anything. Just hide here and let my heart beat for the salmon...and for him.

The sun shines down. Sweat drenches me. My belly twists from hunger. It is too hot to even breathe. I sink down and sleep.

Shouts awake me. I lie in shadow, shivering. It feels like late in the day.

"Join us! Look at all the codfish we have!"

We must be near the shore. That's where my brother says those fish swim. Voices call across the water. The tribal fishermen beg Father to join them. Something lands with a clunk on the wood bottom of the canoe.

"Lures!" Nanolatch screams. "Let's catch some cod!"

The boat leans to one side. I hear a plop as lures sink down into the water. Inside the basket, I stiffen. This is the only basket aboard and surely they will use it if they make a catch.

If.

I squirm myself into a tight ball beneath the seaweed. They won't notice me, I pray.

"There's one!" someone screams. "And another—over there!"

All around me, I hear fish splashing and then the grunts of the men as they spear codfish. Fish land into the bottom of the canoe with a slap. All the while, my heart is a fist in my chest.

"Let me find a place for them," my brother yells.

He pulls off the basket's lid and reaches in. His hand touches my bare flesh. He cries out in surprise.

"What is it?" Father demands.

My father is so close now, that I hear his heavy breathing as he presses against the basket. He leans over with my brother. His black eyes land on mine.

"Get out of there!" Father growls.

The air quivers. Everyone waits. There is no choice. I step out of the basket, covered in seaweed. My brother gasps, his face reddening, remembering he told me about the trip.

But Father pays no attention to my brother. He turns pale, like a fish's underbelly.

"How...how could you do such a thing?" he

thunders at me.

My throat is jammed shut. No thoughts. Just a shiver like ice down my back.

"It is forbidden for any female to come here. They must never visit the Salmon House or see what men do there. The only thing that stops me from disowning you is that you didn't see. You were hidden from their eyes."

But I did see them, and they saw me.

He orders everyone to be still while he chants one last prayer to the salmon. Then he turns to me.

"For the time between one full moon and the next, you will stay in the plankhouse and weave. You will not be allowed on the beach. It is time you learn where you belong—with the women."

Where his voice was full of longing before—sweetness even—when he sang to the salmon, now his voice is flat. I study the lines on my father's face, drawn tight around his mouth.

I will never be the one who lives in his heart. Ever.

When we land, there is nowhere to go except the plankhouse where the women wait in the doorway, leaning out of the raven's mouth, wondering where I disappeared. They whisper when they see me step out of the canoe. Behind me the men stand in a silent huddle. In the house, Grandmother motions me to sit at her right side. I coax Yamunah to lie still. As I rake his hair with a whalebone comb, white clumps of his fur loosen. At first, he does not like it. He only comes close because he loves the warmth of the fire. He is the one thing women can own. Women do not even own their children because they came from the spirits and must be returned to them.

Suddenly my eyes blur as I pick through the whiteness of Yamunah's hair. I should have told Father I was sorry but I could not. It wouldn't be the truth. I rub my hand flat over Yamunah's back. No hair falls loose. I set him free and find another dog. Baskets of white fur overflow by the time I am done.

When I look up, my mother watches me with sorrow-deep eyes, dark as the night sea. Her words are frozen on her lips. Whatever she would have said is a secret now. How gracefully her hands dance, spinning in a circle apart from me. I cannot join her there.

At her loom, my mother works into her blanket a new pattern, drawn by my father called, "A Thousand Salmon Running." It is a magic totem to call the salmon back into the rivers. To watch my mother is to be placed under a spell. Her slim, bare arms dance in the air, running smoothly over the wool like water over a waterfall. Red wool from boiled alder bark. Brown from hemlock. Yellow from lichen. The salmon she weaves are bright red and leaping. Beneath her hands grow the salmon and their Salmon House beneath the sea.

One winter or more will pass before her blanket is woven. When it is done, it will hang on our walls.

When other tribes visit at potlatch, their mouths
will drop open at the beauty of our blankets—hung
side by side, our walls swimming with salmon. The
more blankets the women weave, the wealthier our
tribe appears.

All women spin, even the michimis. These are
women who know how to spice a kettle of fish stew
with just the right pinch of dulse and when to pull
the smoking salmon out of the coals. They can quiet
a screaming infant and dress a warrior's wounds. But
there is no beauty in their hands, like my mother's,
only calluses.

They gossip about me, I am sure. Perhaps they
are predicting when I will be wed and what price my
suitor will offer for me, paid in gleaming copper.
The women wonder if my bridegroom will be as
strong as my brother is. As lean and tall, dark
skinned, and just as rich.

These women remind me of sea turtles, the way
their eyes turn to watch me. Their bodies sag in layers of thick skin like whale blubber. They do not
budge unless they have to. They are content to tug
at yarn, forcing it to spin in the exact pattern of
their great-grandmothers before them.

Shall I shock them and say that I have been
where no female is allowed, and still the Salmon
House spins? These men are wrong, I would say, but
they all believe I did a forbidden thing.

The air in this smoky hut chokes me. A single
ray of pearl-gray light peeks in through the rooftop.

If only there was a breeze of sea-salt air to fill my lungs.

If I had been born male, I would not sit here with this useless dog. Forever squatting, folding my legs beneath me. Combing all winter long. I would be up the cliffside in a moment.

I am prey, caught in a spider's web. Every time the spider creeps, he makes me whirl around and around. My life is spinning without me. I cling to the web with my hands and feet.

I look for a place to leap.

TSETSEKA
TIME WHEN NOTHING IS REAL

NOH

Don't you ever, you up in the sky,
don't you ever get tired
of having the clouds between you and us?

All day Nana peeks through the cracks in the cedar walls, and chants. Once she recognized the slightest shifting of gray. Silver on the horizon. The blue-gray of rain. The dimming gray of storms approaching. Trapped behind walls, she gives up hope of ever seeing the sunshine. Outside, the wind rushes through the empty planks in the burial grounds.

Like smoke, the girl's mind roams everywhere. Yet her body seems wrapped in a
cocoon, tightly spun. She wishes to crawl to
her hiding place high on the cliffs and never
leave. But she remembers to shift her fingers to
spin. Grandmother's hands sometimes touch
hers, firmly guiding them.

Only at night, wrapped in the safety of darkness, does she whisper to me. There is no one
else to tell. No one who will listen to a girl who
has broken taboos. Although I don't speak back,
I pull her toward me with my thoughts. Her
eyes study me, sinking her spirit down into me.
She forgets everything and sleeps. Sometimes,
when no one is looking, I smooth her hair gently as her mother used to do.

In wintertime, spirits are closer to earth. Winter,
when the tribe is still—that's when the spirits
fly. Spirits roll in with the fog, and linger. Night
falls early. Outside the sea tosses and turns,
swishes and sways. It never sleeps. Its breath of
salt blows through our door. Its dampness
crawls into our plankhouse and pries beneath
our mats.

Inside it is warm and dry where we all settle
at night. Red flames leap. Shadows dance on the
ceiling as the young ones huddle near the fire.

Nanolatch stretches out on his stomach,

propping his chin in his hands. I squat opposite him, by his sister's side. He looks from face to face until his eyes land on mine. Shilka sits down between us and the boy's gaze shifts. Then he stares at me again as if he and I are alone in the plankhouse. My heart pounds. His gaze is the same as his touch, which I felt just once, hot as summer sun. Slowly I turn my head. All the adults gather in a far corner, talking. No one sees us.

His eyes look so deeply into me, I am lost. I feel the boy's spirit enter me. I am filled with his thoughts, his wonderings.

You are a shaman. I should be afraid of you. But I want to know all about you. You won't say one word to me. Please tell me who you are.

The sound of Shilka's hoarse voice jolts us. We both turn our heads toward the shaman. He storytalks. His eyes shine like obsidians as he rocks back and forth, remembering.

"There was a time when your great-great-grandfather, the chief, was sick. He could not get out of bed. Fever. Red scratches on his face. Strong Ekas had hold of him. The shaman was called in. Smelled him. He said the Ekas stole the chief's soul and were running to the river to drown it. The chief would die. So the shaman grabbed a soulcatcher quick."

Shilka rattles his ancient soulcatcher, carved

out of cedar with a raven head at both ends. He blows through it, scattering spit over all our faces. We lean back but soon press forward again. I dare not lift my eyes. My cheeks feel hot. The boy still stares.

Shilka continues. "The shaman ran to the river, warriors at his heels. He held the soulcatcher behind his back and crooned softly to the Ekas. The warriors held their breath. The shaman chanted, his lips never still. His mouth opened wide into a smile. Out from its hiding place, the soulcatcher jumped and snapped back the soul. He ran all the way back to the plankhouse with it. Your great-great-grandfather lay like a dead man. The shaman set the soulcatcher on his mouth and blew into it. The chief took a deep breath. His chest filled higher and higher. His soul flew back into his chest. He lived for many long years."

Shilka shakes the soulcatcher at us. The youngest jerk back.

"Tell us more," Raven Sun begs.

Shilka grimaces, showing his black gums. The children listen until they can no longer sit up. Some I carry to their sleeping spots. The rest crawl beneath mats. They shut their eyes, listening, falling into their dreams. Even Nanolatch and his sister lie, quiet.

I wonder why Shilka tells the story on this winter night. Warnings must play in his mind.

Or...a vision perhaps? That's when all the hairs on the back of my neck rise up. The shaman must sense the Ekas approaching, and yet he gives no warnings. There will be no way to stop them unless the tribe is prepared.

I crawl over to where the twins have fallen asleep, their heads still tilted, waiting to hear more. The boy's fists are clenched. The girl sleepwalks day and night.

A voice enters me, splitting through my head.

It is the twins we want.

A shadow flies by, darkening the ceiling with its wings. Something comes and goes from this room. Ekas will try to stop them from becoming who they are.

I must tell them.

I tried to push the girl before, force her out where she was not ready to go. But now I must be gentle, so quiet, she will not guess I am near.

So I will send them dreams. Winter is the time when sleep is deep. Spirits touch down in our dreams. If we listen closely, we will hear them speak.

Let me spin dreams in their minds. Dark warnings to be careful.

I bend over Nana's ear and blow an ancient chant into it—Salish words of protection. *Keep watch!* Her face draws tight and her mouth falls open. She has heard my foretelling.

I creep over to Nanolatch. How I wish to trace that square, hard chin and the bluntness of his cheekbones with my fingertips. But I dare not wake him. Instead, I blow the chant again until it shimmers all through his body with a trembling that matches my own.

The twins listen as a spirit does, without a body, drifting to the land of their ancestors.

Where the
Salmon Leap

CHAPTER 14

Shadow of the Thunderbird

NANOLATCH

The elders meditate in a circle around us before we leave. Their bodies are thin, their skin stretched tightly over their bones. No one waves. Grandmother is a speck on the sand as we head across sea. Each year she shrinks, curving to the ground like a willow branch. All her chants never drew one salmon upstream.

We leave for upriver when it is already summer, after a wild rainstorm. We can wait no longer, Father says. The spring brought little rain. This storm might still allow us to ride up the river.

I look away from the plankhouses. I tell myself everything is ahead of me. I will meet it with a

stroke. After all the fishing in the whitecaps beside
Second Uncle, Father says I am ready for this journey. My whole body strains against the current
pushing us toward the shore. Drummers beat a
rhythm to quicken our pace.

"The sea is a wild animal you must tame so it
lets you ride its back," Father warns me. "Too tame,
and the ride will be slow. Too wild, and it will
throw you overboard."

"How will I know what to do?" I call over to
him.

"Watch the water. Think of nothing but the current. It will tell you what has to be done. It changes
from moment to moment. You must be ready to
shift with it."

And so I watch. My hips pull out of their joints.
My back is plank straight. My arms tighten into
bone. The sea and I curve together. I could paddle
like this forever.

Before nightfall, we reach the river. It twists,
narrow and shallow, like a snake. We must lift our
canoes instead of riding. The river runs like that,
Father says, never the same river from year to year.
But just as we round a bend in the river, Thunderbird flies over our heads. Its shadow stains the water
black. It is said that, with one rustle of his wings,
somewhere thunder rolls.

Shilka points his staff for the fishermen to turn
right, but it is too late. All our canoes float under
the wide-open wings of Thunderbird. Pass under its

night-dark shadow.

"Pull to shore," Shilka screams. "We are cursed!"

The shaman's face is a bunched-up storm cloud. He orders us to kneel on rock while he pours water over our bowed heads. Dried bone charms rattle in the air. No one speaks. The sun sets, leaving us in shadow. A chill rushes through me, as if I had plunged into icy water.

We reach upriver soon after, not eating. We set up camp and sleep.

In the morning, I race to the riverbank with uncle's harpoon. With it, I believe I have the power to catch anything. The waterfall is higher and louder than ever, full of snowmelt. But no fish swim. The men struggle to dip the salmon trap into the water. We return at dusk, to cricket chirps and owl hoots...but no fish. Each night, darkness swallows us. And still there is no Chinook or sockeye run. Their season is passing. Shilka paces in and out of the woods, muttering chants.

Every time I remember the curse, I think how I should have swerved the canoe out of Thunderbird's reach, and I tighten my fists. Waves of heat flush my chest. I feel like screaming at Father. If I had been trained from the first as a warrior, I would have seen Thunderbird!

I would have been so sharp, my eyes on the water, alert to everything around me. But the current amazed me—its voice so wild, I could barely hold on. I could have beaten my chest, or anyone who came near me.

I clench my jaw for fear I will yell.

I shoot my words like arrows to sting Nana. I mock her slowness, laughing at her legs, like wooden logs, while mine leap high as a partridge. I could beat her at anything, and that is all I wish to do now.

When Noh passes, I will not look at her. I want to brush those ash lines from her face. She walks in our midst, marked like that. It makes me want to scream out the truth. The curse we set upon her tribe marks us all.

The summer days pass. Father says we will wait a little longer for the next run to come. I am so bored that I trail my sister around. Early one morning, Nana goes to the river when everyone still sleeps. Secretly, she sneaks there, singing to the salmon, as we were taught. Her voice rises high and sweet above the roar of the waterfall. Without a word, I stretch out beside her and dangle my fingers in the cool water. When she stops singing, I open my eyes. A flutter of blue and silver flashes by.

A pink salmon run.

GIVING RAIN AWAITING THUNDER

NANA

A thin pink salmon leaps, but the force of the
waterfall throws him spinning back. He lifts
ten feet up, higher than I have seen any fish
jump, and still he falls back down. One by one,
the other salmon jump, iridescent in the misty
morning air. The lead salmon waits.

Nanolatch runs to awaken the tribe. It is too
late to give him warning. To tell him about the
dark whisperings that echoed in my sleep
before we left our village. When the fishermen
rush in, I feel a tug at my heart. All the fish
safely jump. It is the moment. The lead salmon
leaps. Muscles burst in his chest. His neck
stretches out flat. This time, I hope, he will
rise another foot higher. I hold my breath,
watching him. But Father's spear zings past.
The fish flops back into the pool, the sharp
bone point through his back.

A cry falls from my throat in that moment,
the last moment the salmon does not have. All
my words are trapped inside, words I would
have spilled if I had been allowed. Everything I
know is left unsaid, twisting within me. My
brother turns his head and sees my face,
soaked with tears.

Too late.

The pink salmon is no more. No one mourns his passing but me. No one hears his singing but me. His flesh is soft and sweet and drives all the fishermen back to the river.

During a salmon run, I cannot keep my eyes off Nanolatch. He leaps as high as a young deer. Light. Four hands taller. Moving like wind. One moment behind me, running, then flying ten feet ahead of me. His harpoon flies through the air like an arrow. Fish flip back into the pool. Underwater, the trap fills. Racks are stretched with drying salmon. My brother is lit up like the sun, his smile dazzling. Even Noh pauses at her work to admire him. It is as if some spirit possesses him. He is not known to any of us.

Sometimes I notice Father and Second Uncle, heads together, whispering, their eyes on me. Many moons ago, Father said he made a plan with the Nootkas. *I'd rather stay here with you.* That's what I'd tell him if we spoke as father and daughter. When he went to war, when we lost the salmon, he turned away. But, before that, I was always a girl who went her own way. He didn't approve. If only I could save the salmon, we could be close again.

No one expects much of me or cares what I do upriver. I pick salal berries in the woods. I have grown in the past year. My hips swell and soften, as does my chest. I am smaller and rounder than my brother is. I am changing without my wanting to. My body is becoming someone else's.

Noh passes with her load of baskets. My soul roams toward her like a cloud, loaded with the burden of my grayness. I spill my complaints like rain. I speak to her as if she understands my language.

"I am a Salmon Twin," I tell her. "I should look different from soft Kwakiutl women who spin all winter long. Surely there is something special I must do, like Nanolatch. But there is no sign."

Noh drops her baskets and squats down beside me. She leans her head to one side. Just her eyes listen, growing wide.

"I have this one spark of memory but I do not know what it means," I tell her. "I was here with my brother and both of us were blessed. Only my brother has found his Way. My Way is slippery as fog."

There is something new in Noh's eyes. Inside them, I can feel my own pain reflected, as the sea does when you bend close to peer into it. It's as if she gathers all the rain from me so I can breathe again.

Nearby, water trickles over rock. The sound calms me. Later I will swim, light and slippery. My body tingles all night long after a swim.

Lightness floats inside me. I walk on air. If only I could swim now. I would swim away from what edges in close upriver, riding behind Thunderbird's wings. The crack of thunder will come soon. It always follows in his trail.

One night, sleep pulls me down like a drug. Covers me in waves of dreams. Drags me down to the underworld. I dream of a fish with one huge eye watching me. Its eye grows bigger and bigger, until all I see is its eye. I swim after him. He turns to look back at me, and becomes Thunderbird. He opens his mouth wide and grabs all our belongings. I chase after him but he swims so far ahead of me, I cannot catch up. Before he lifts up into the air, I see the pure white of his straight teeth. The raven blackness of his sleek long hair. His thick muscled neck. His laughter echoes across miles and miles of river water.

I awaken, screaming.

CHAPTER 15

His Wings Beating Down

NANOLATCH

In the grayness of early morning, fishermen dart like shadows across camp. A hundred feet drum the ground. I run after them. The fishermen surround the drying racks. They are bone dry. The fish we stretched upon them this summer have vanished.

"Someone has stolen the fish!" Head Fisherman yells.

"Who could have done this?" screams a fishwife.

"Another tribe," guesses Second Uncle. "Jealous of our good catch."

"Search around camp for their trail," Father commands.

We spread out along the mountain paths but find

no sign of anyone. Not one plant has been disturbed. Shilka awaits us at the river with his legs planted wide apart. He glares from one fisherman to another. "Fools! Did you find a trail? No! For you cannot see them or hear them. You have no power to find the Ekas. Thunderbird warned us. The spirits have flown away and the salmon will not swim here."

The fishermen lower their eyes to the ground.

"You must guard the camp. Protect the catch each night. Watch the Salmon Twins," Shilka points his staff at my sister and me. "They are the ones who can save the salmon. Never leave the twins alone by the river."

A chill runs through me like a cold current at the bottom of the sea. I hold myself unflinching, as Kwakiutls are taught to do. It is then that I remember when we captured the first salmon of the season. My sister gasped, quick tears smearing her face. She alone felt the curse nearby.

The men leave to hunt deer in the woods. One fisherman stands guard over Nana and me, a spear across his folded arms.

My sister's eyes are shadowy, full of dimness— like rain clouds.

"The Ekas have cursed us," I tell her. "When we call by the river, the salmon do not come as they did on our first visit."

"The salmon are disappearing, but they still come," she insists. "We must try again. Let's call them together so they will not be afraid."

Nana tugs at my arm but I can't stay there. I'd rather hunt with the men. I trail the murmur of the men's voices until I find them. Father walks in the lead, the lines around his mouth deep and turned down. The silence of the dark mountains wraps around him.

"Don't leave your sister alone," he warns me. "No matter how much you are tempted to go somewhere, stay with her. Go back now."

All I can do is pace by the river. Catch the few fish passing by. I won't keep the silent watch my sister does, her eyes upon the water. The salmon won't return that way. My harpoon is always by my side.

Shilka insists we leave. On the last day we swim beneath the waterfall. The pool numbs us like snow water. I leap into the waterfall like a fish. It pushes me back. I scream a warrior's cry at the top of my lungs to scare the Ekas away. But my sister is swept back, twirled underwater, swirled in circles. She plunges to the surface, gasping. Nana splashes out when she sees Father come. She rushes to him. I haven't seen them together since our journey to the Salmon House.

Her voice drifts over to me. "Leave me here. By spring, the salmon will be waiting for you."

Father shakes his head. "The snow will come, and the bitter cold. But there are worse dangers. You must come home with us."

My father loads the canoes beside the fishermen without another word. He moves like a shadow, stiff and dark. It is the way he acted at the Salmon House. He looks up when my sister cries out but remains silent.

"The salmon need to hear my voice," Nana insists. "Now!"

Her words are like the cry of the lead salmon, which never scaled the waterfall but fell dead with a spear through its back. Even Noh stands still, listening. Her face is as mournful as my sister's.

There are no answers to the elders' questions when we return. The worry grows in their red-rimmed eyes. I cast my glance to the sand as we step ashore and drop six baskets of pink salmon down at their feet. I do not want to see the darkness in their eyes, wondering why our tribe must suffer this winter.

STANDING STILL

NOH

She is like a fish out of water.

Work she does not feel like doing. Salmon-berries to be picked while they are plump and juicy. Mountain herbs to be gathered. And there are stinging looks from Nanolatch that pinch her like poison arrows.

She does not know where she belongs.

She longs only to stand by the river's edge. Remind the salmon of their journey up this river. River of their birth. River of their death. She promises them that some will safely reach the breeding grounds.

If they do not come, the salmon will disappear.

She stands by the river and the salmon do not run. She faces downstream to the sea and calls. The words scratch in her throat like dry bones.

And still they do not come.

She drops her head and stands alone by the river, heavy as stone. She has lost all her brothers.

She stands still.

As I do, not knowing what else can be done.

Place of Mists

CHAPTER 16

Forever Looking at Me

NANA

Grandmother meets me on the beach for our morning training. Each day, we sit in the Ceremonial House for a lesson on stilling the mind. I can never follow her directions. Grandmother's shoulders droop, more than I remember. You can see each and every bone in her body.

"You are thirteen. Next year is your Initiation. After two years of training, you cannot sit still at either meditation or spinning." She sighs. "I fear you will not discover in time the treasures that are inside you. You must find what makes you so restless."

"What treasures could be inside me?"

"Come," she invites. "Let's sit."

So we begin. I sit straight, my back as flat as hers, while I fold my legs beneath me. The fire is unlit and the wind pushes behind us. Dampness crawls in, creeping over my skin. I gather my cedar cape tightly around my chest.

"Watch the breath," she instructs. "Follow it. Do not budge if a thought comes."

The sea's breath blows through the walls, whistling haunted tunes. My thoughts roam every-where—thin wisps of smoke.

Grandmother's eyes are closed but still she knows everything, even what I am thinking. "Let your thoughts drift to sea. Let them pass by."

"My mind wants to go with them, Grandmother. Besides, what would I be without my thoughts?"

"You would be yourself, whom you are most afraid to be."

Again we sit in stillness. Now and then I peek to see if she has stirred. But she sits so still, as if she is not there at all.

My mind drifts with the wind, up to the cliffs where I long to be. I squirm as if a million mosqui-toes have lit on my bare skin. *Nanolatch does not have to sit still. He is out on the sea just now, lov-ing every minute of it. Males can do as they wish.*

Grandmother turns toward me. "Your breath was quick just now. Have you found what tosses your mind in so many places?"

"I am afraid," I confess to her, "that I will never

find my place as my brother does."

She shakes her wispy gray head. "His Way is not yours. He takes the expected path. Yours will open if you listen."

I stretch my legs out, but she holds hers firm. "You must push past your feelings. Sit in stillness. Face your fears. If you don't learn now, evil will take you at your Initiation. It waits all around, trying to disturb us as it did the Salmon House. Hold fast!"

Again she straightens her back and closes her eyes. The sea's roar fills the room and my own breath joins it, like the two are one, moving in and out. After awhile I do not think. My breath moves by itself. The thoughts are pieces now. An eagle's slow circle. The deep blue sea. Then nothing.

A thousand salmon eyes dance in front of me. Shimmering as if they are underwater. Moving through salt cold water. So deep, farther out than I have ever been. I follow them, keeping pace, flicking my body as if I have a tail and fins. Wooden totem poles arise, towering red in front of me. It is the Salmon House beneath the sea. Glittering with jewels. Full of fish that splash a path for me to enter.

I am home.

When I finally open my eyes, Grandmother is staring at me.

"You have found a treasure, Nana—a vision. Keep it secret. But tell me, will you go back there?"

"If I can, Grandmother. If I remember how."

"Once you have been there," she smiles, "you

will always long to return. Now, go outside and greet the day."

I skip out of the Ceremonial House, passing by Noh, who carries kindling from the forest. I set my finger to my lips. She nods. Up we climb, pressing into shadow, beneath the limbs of the firs. We rest at the top of the cliff with our hearts pounding wildly against the ground.

Noh follows me now with just a sign. She never spills my secrets. From the cliff we both look down at the fishwives' daughters surrounding my brother on the beach in low tide.

"How they flock to him like gulls to fish," I mock. "Can you hear them squawking all the way up here?"

Noh doesn't laugh with me. She keeps her eyes on the girls, who surround my brother in an admiring circle. In their midst, Nanolatch bends to his work, emptying nets of flounder from the bay.

"As the chief's son, he won't be allowed to choose his bride, just as I can't chose a husband," I tell her. "A chief's son must wed another chief's daughter. But if a boy is still unwed when he becomes a chief, then he has a choice. He can pick any girl from any tribe, and she will be honored to be his wife."

Noh looks at me then, her eyes wide.

"But that won't happen. Father will choose his bride," I continue. "There are none here who will do. Father will look elsewhere—to another tribe."

Noh turns her back on the beach below. She
squats, hugging her knees to her chest, rocking back
and forth. She will not look at me again.

But then we hear the guard shout from the cliff.
Out on the whitecaps, canoes appear in the mist.
Fifteen of them. The sight stops my heart. Who rides
in them, I do not know. We should both be down
there to find out. Slaves should surround my father,
protecting him. Noh is the first to budge, scrambling
down without me. Warriors rush to the beach,
spears in hand. Fishermen drag canoes across the
sand. Father breaks through them, holding his hands
up.

Everyone and everything on the sand below is
suddenly still.

As I scurry down, the warriors lower their spears
and turn away. I hear the guard yell, "Nootkas!" to
all the village. The name catches me by surprise.
Then I see the women carrying blankets into the
Ceremonial House. There must be a ceremony soon,
although no one told me. By the time I reach the
beach, Noh's bundle of wood is flying up in the air.
Father, spear in hand, strikes her down. Noh covers
her head with her arms. Blood drips from her face.

"How can I boast of my daughter to the
Nootkas?" Father yells. "They arrive and you don't
know where she hides. You are worthless! Nothing!
A ghost! You cannot keep track of her for a few
hours."

"Here I am, Father!" I call out.

He whirls around. "Go to your mother right
now. You need to bathe and dress for the ceremony."
I hesitate on the sand, looking down at Noh. She
is a bundle, not a girl anymore, but a slave again. I
reach down to help her up.

"Go!" thunders Father.

And I run. With each step, I feel the tears drop
down on my bare feet. I am betrayed. Not by a slave,
as I feared, but by my own father. He has set a trap
for me. It will open tonight. I, in my dress of pink
salmon, swirling, will face his plans.

Inside the plankhouse my mother dries my face
at once. Her fingers touch me so softly, as if she will
never see me again. She studies me like I am a treasure to admire. It is a lingering look, like a farewell.

Inside the Winter Ceremonial House, slaves fling
candlefish oil into the fire. Flames splash blood red.
The Nootkas cheer, their eyes glowing. So many
candlefish just thrown away—a sign of our wealth.
Little does the tribe care now the long days it took
to catch and boil them down. Besides, we are not
rich anymore, without our salmon catch.

"This is my daughter," Father announces to the
Nootka chief. "She will enter her Initiation next
winter and then be ready to wed."

I am weighed like a slab of salmon. Nootka eyes
swallow my roundness, a sign of womanhood. My
soft breasts. Wide, muscled shoulders from climbing.
My bewildered face. They do not care for beauty, I

have heard the fishwives murmur, only status. I am
a catch, the biggest fish in the tribal sea, the daughter of the chief. Circles of abalone shells wound
around and around my neck, choking me.

"What will you offer us for her?" Father
demands.

"Ten coppers and two war canoes," the Nootka
chief says.

"She is our only daughter. Such a prize she is,"
announces my father. "How can I just give her away
to another tribe?"

"We will welcome her as one of our own," the
Nootka chief responds.

He claps his hands while his slaves carry in
mounds of marmot and bearskin. They heap baskets
of wool and more woven blankets than we can
count.

Father gleams. "We accept. Three war canoes
will we carve especially for you. My very own copper, handed down by the ancestors, will be yours
too. The marriage will take place at the end of next
winter, before fishing. Your royal son will wed her."

The young son of the Nootka chief glances at me
out of the side of his eyes, like a spy fish. His face is
oily and dark, as if he drank seal oil. All evening, he
burps like a bear, snorting his food down. He does
not look me full in the face so I can see his soul and
he can see mine. I would never trust such a boy.

I do not smile the whole night of the betrothal
ceremony. Father sits and laughs with the Nootkas.

He never looks my way. I will soon be gone and he will not even miss me. When my brother turns my way, I toss my head. I won't let him know how I twist inside, like a hooked fish, unable to swim away.

Not one word do I say to anyone except Grandmother. She watched me closely during the speeches. When the delicacies are passed around, roasted deer meat, I whisper in her ear.

"Is this what you meant this morning when you said there is not much time left for me?"

Grandmother nods. "You must learn now. It will save you."

"Will it save me from the Nootka's son?"

She pauses. "If you know who you are, you can change your destiny. But the Way may wish to carry you elsewhere."

I beg her then to tell me the potion to dress Noh's wound.

"In the black drum in the Big House. The herbs in the deer pouch," she tells me. "Wet them and press them to her cut."

As the men sit in circles and talk, I slip out. The herbs are where Grandmother says and I prepare them as she instructs. Then I creep behind the totem poles on the beach, where I know she will be. Behind one, Noh has dropped to the sand like a heavy sack. Dried blood marks her cheek, a long wound sliced by Father's spear. It will likely leave a scar. I brush her hair back. I call her name over and over, but she does not answer me.

I have seen her like this before, staring blankly. I wonder where she goes when she drifts, like smoke you can't hold onto. I worry she is one of the Spiritless Ones. I pray it is not so, that she still lives somewhere inside herself in spite of all she has lost.

I prop her up against a totem pole and press the poultice of herbs to her cheek. The hemlock licks her wound with its own bite. She winces and then sinks back, her dark face so lost, so mournful. I think, though I am a chief's daughter, I am just like Noh.

To be female in this village is to be a slave to men's demands. It is to have our spirits slashed before they have begun to soar.

CHAPTER 17

Spirit Sent

NOH

The cut slices through my soul. It goes whirling into smoke, into shadow, through the icy air back in time. Countless ravens fly above me.

The boy leaps, firstborn son. The girl arrives later, with her grandmother's coaxing. She is secondborn, a daughter. All the ancestors of the Raven Clan lean into the world to look.

Through memory, the girl will awaken. In the time of their Initiation, both will pass to another place.

The firmness of the totem pole presses against my shoulder. Upon my wound are the sting of herbs and the bite of damp sea air. Then the touch of wrinkled hands, sending warmth to ease my shivering.

"Nana sent me, Noh. You would not move and she could not carry you. You must come inside. It is late."

Flies on Wind strokes my hair, smoothing it out of my face. She studies my face.

"A vision burns in your eyes," she says. "You have drifted back to your childhood. You are one who is becoming a shaman."

I shake my head wildly. Grandmother is wrong. She only guesses what I hoped to be, what I cannot be now. Here they call me ghost, not a girl. I keep silent and give no answer, as I have vowed. I will tell her nothing of this vision.

Grandmother's thoughts shoot at me, clear and loud.

Shush! We will speak with our minds, not our voices. Surely you know how to do that. You can keep your vow of silence until the time when you must speak out.

Her thoughts touch me deeply, making me wish to confess everything. Grandmother continues. *You came to us with a grizzly bear necklace around your neck—sign of an initiated shaman.*

But—I don't know how it came! It belonged to my mother.

Think back. What happened after the battle in your village?

I remembered the bloody bodies on the sand, and then I was in the speeding Kwakiutl canoe. I was not alive or dead. I drifted in the Country of the Ghosts. All the Salish dead came to visit me. How I longed to go with them.

Who else was there? Grandmother presses me to tell more.

Why, my mother, Wind Tamer. I waited for her to bring me with her. But instead, she came quite close and touched me here, around my neck.

I gasp, feeling the exact spot where the necklace was. Grandmother's eyes, sunken specks beneath the folds of her eyelids, pop open. The light in them shines brighter than any sun.

Your mother gave you the necklace. That death journey was your Initiation. You did not wander in the woods as most children your age do. Instead, the battle changed you into a shaman. That day, the child in you died.

But, I have awaited my guardian spirit. None came to help me.

Flies on Wind sighs. *You walk alone, the most difficult path of all, part of the test of becoming a shaman. You must continue to develop to your fullness. When you are ready, your guardian spirit will appear. But it is not time yet.*

Again I shake my head. *I have no powers as my mother did, to heal the sick and tame the wind.*

Your powers are different than hers, Noh. Look to the burial ground— our fallen warriors sleep and no longer haunt the land of the living. Look to Nanolatch—his power grows.

I did not know what I was doing. It was just a trick.

You control the ghosts still. They would rise if not for you. You are Spirit Sent. Chosen before your birth to follow a shaman's path.

I almost cry aloud all the questions burning my soul. I tell her of the vision then, much as I told my mother all those years ago, without receiving an answer then.

Grandmother nods. *The two who came to you are my twin grandchildren. They appeared to ask your help.*

I sit straight up. A current rips through me like a lightning rod. I never knew that anyone guessed my secret. The twins are the ones to whom I was sent. I had no choice but to come. I was called.

Why was I sent here? I gasp.

Grandmother smiles. *My granddaughter is alone, like you. She is one who needs a friend. You accept her. You want her to become who she was meant to be. That is what a friend does.*

I plead with her. *But I have done a calling ceremony and sent her dreams, and still the twins are split apart. The girl seems so lost. What more can I do?*

Stay by her. Tie Nanolatch to you, however you

*can. You will need his help. Watch and listen. Be
ready.*

For what, Grandmother?

*To slip between – be a link between the living
and the living this time.*

All is twirling inside me, tossing like waves.
Grandmother pulls me from the Land of the Ghosts.
No longer does the wound pound in my face. Arm
in arm, we walk back to the Ceremonial House. In
that moment she feels like my own grandmother,
the one I left behind in Salish land.

Inside I sink down at Nana's feet. How I wish to
sit up all night and talk to her, but she is asleep.
Besides, she would be afraid to hear what I would
tell her. The vision might frighten her.

Beside the fire Nanolatch stirs, awakening, as if
I had called him. I look right into his eyes. Grandmother said I will need his help. He is the one I will
tell everything to. He will return to his sister then.
But, around us, the Nootkas still talk with the
chief.

I motion to Nanolatch with signs, as I have seen
the fishermen do, raising my head, and turning
away to announce a meeting. I tuck my finger
beneath my thumb and point to the eastern sky
where the sun will rise tomorrow. Then I spread my
fingers like waves for the beach.

His face softens, countless yearnings passing
over it. I want to reach out to touch his lips, but I
must wait. No one must know. No one must see.

Nanolatch gives me his answer. He places his hands behind his back—a sign.

I will go there.

TURNING AWAY

NANOLATCH

I did not sleep the whole night. My heart was pumping fast and nothing I could do would still it.

The blackness now shifts. Soon it will be dawn. Everywhere in the Ceremonial House, guests sleep. Beside me, my sister tosses on her mat. She and I seem to be at war, villages apart. Where I roam, she cannot follow. Besides, her way is foretold. She will depart with the Nootka's son and never be part of us again. That boy is no warrior. He is still a child, just ten years old. Last night I heard him sobbing in the dark, begging to go home to his mother. I can hardly believe my sister wishes to go with him. Her lips hold back what once she would have shared with me. She turns away, her looks cutting the air like spears.

At my sister's feet, Noh curls up. Late last night, for the first time, she told me with her gestures, that she must see me alone. It startled me, for she spoke in the sign language

only fishermen use among themselves. Noh
has no words. Only those looks that slide from
her dark eyes, sweeping over me. She examines
every detail of my features for clues of what I
hide within. Her glance brushes over my bare
chest, lingers on my lips, then shifting, stares
boldly into my eyes. My secrets rush toward
her like the tides.

One lives who grasps my secret longings.
She, who others have made a slave, is able to
see me better than my father, certainly more
than my sister.

Suddenly Noh stirs on her mat, stretching to
greet the new day. I press my face flat into the
ground, wondering what she will do. My heart
pounds in my ears and I fear she will hear it.
She crawls straight to my mat. I feel her touch
tremble all through me. A light touch of her
hand on my hair as she passes by. And then she
hurries out, swallowed by the Raven's mouth.

Something in my chest rips apart. How can I
let Noh drift here when she belongs elsewhere?
My own father and uncle brought her here. I
cannot go against them. But in the ash that
darkens her cheeks, I trace how Kwakiutl
spears sharpened the curse. They dug it deeper
into our own flesh. Beneath our skin, our souls
are etched in ash forever, like hers. We are all
in mourning for what we have lost.

I look up to the smoke hole where the sky

shifts to pink. Soon the sun will rise. Noh waits. But I will not go. I will not touch her thick shiny hair, or ever know if she has a voice to speak. I must turn from this girl before I spill out what I vowed my uncle I would never tell.

It will only stir up trouble if she knew. She may run off, or worse, cast a spell on us, as I believe she could. If she was clever enough to guess the fishermen's secret language, she knows much more about us.

I must break with the past forever. Leave my sister behind. Kill the one I was. Bury this smoldering that eats at my heart every time Noh passes by.

There is nothing I can do except follow this one path—be the one First Uncle wished me to be.

Until I do that, I am nothing.

CHAPTER 18

Leaping from Home

NANA

Nanolatch moves out.

Gone.

He leaves behind his basket of stones. He takes only his garments.

He will live at Second Uncle's house to begin the year of his apprenticeship. Only when he marries will he return to my father's house.

A landslide falls between Nanolatch and me, cliff high, so we seem to live in separate villages. He no longer stretches out on the sand beside me, planning what we will do upriver. I cannot watch his face light up with dreams as he sleeps by the evening fire.

He gives up the ways of a child. He collects no stones, no feathers. And he gives up me—his sister.

As the days pass, he follows in my uncle's shadow and does his bidding.

There are plans for me as well.

Noh and I gather herbs from the cliffside. Beneath us, the sea licks the shore as it breathes in and out, pulling far away, then returning. Outside, the world seems wide. But in the afternoon, the women call me away from the sparkling sea.

"You will spin with me this fall," Grandmother seats me beside her, drawing me against her wrinkled skin. "Little by little, we will teach you weaving. You will gather herbs and dye wool."

"You will follow my path," announces my mother.

She stands erect at her loom. Her hands are never still. Her breath catches at times when her eyes stray to me. All the words she could have said are spinning in the air, away from us. She dares not question Father's plans.

Indoors, it is smoky from the fire. Even in the middle of the day, it seems like night. One ray of sunshine falls down from the hole in the ceiling. We all crowd under it to spin and weave. My thoughts drift in the endless fog. Grandmother taps my shoulder to bring my mind back from wandering.

We brew dye with the wool in a steamy pot over the fire, until yellow stains it like sunshine. Until red soaks it like blood. Until brown blows through it

like dirt. We hang it from the walls to dry. It will
flap above our heads endless winter days.

Grandmother and I sit down to twist wool onto
the spindle. She has woven for forty-five long winters. Her hands are twisted like tree roots. A gray
film clouds her eyes. She feels with her hands. She
listens with her fingers, never missing a strand.

"Pull the wool gently between both your hands,
Nana." Her voice is sharp and thin as wind. "Pull it
until you feel it is stretched enough. It must be
stretched to give it strength. But if you yank too
hard, it will break."

The wool snaps in two. I pick up another piece.
Over and over again, it tears.

"Listen to the wool, Nana." She tilts her head.
"It makes a sound when it is ready. Music. Like
a bowstring drawn tight."

We spend whole days inside. The wool rubs
against my hands, scraping them raw. Outside, I do
not know if the sun has broken through or if the fog
is still thick.

When the fishermen land at dusk, the spell of
weaving that has fallen over the women breaks like
an overstretched spider web. The fishwives rise to
prepare the day's catch. I dive out the door, hoping
to catch a glimpse of Nanolatch, back from the day's
hunt. He will have time to himself before nightfall. I
scan the shoreline. Empty. My footsteps freeze on
the sand. High upon the cliff, he stands.

Nanolatch.

Alone, he looks out to sea as if he is already miles away. Tomorrow is his fasting trial—the first test of manhood. My uncle will leave him in a cave on the mountainside for five days without food, water or fire. I want to say goodbye to my brother on his way to becoming a man so soon, in just five days. But if I climb up, I will be a shadow beside him.

I walk the shore below with a fire that burns in my belly. The fire of remembering. Far out on the sea, where the Salmon House is, a dim glow pulses.

*

Six days later I weave at the loom.

"Draw your thread straight down," my mother directs me. "Keep your wrist loose. Don't tighten your arm!"

It snaps between my fingers. My mother must pull out all the threads and start again. One tie in the wool will weaken the whole blanket.

"The wool will give when it is gently pulled," Grandmother says. "Feel how it tells you when you have stretched it enough."

She pats my head just as she did when I was little. Both my hands ache. They feel like two left hands, too big for weaving. The wool has carved red scratches that sting my flesh. I bow my head and weave the day away.

The yell awakens us. A deep boom from the

cliffs. We all rush to the door of the plankhouse, even my bent grandmother. Noh follows at our heels on tiptoe.

Nanolatch. Leaner than when he left but full of fire.

He leaps down the cliff, screaming at the top of his lungs. His war cries echo off the red cliffs and fly throughout the village.

We all wait in the doorway—the women of his family.

Grandmother. Mother. Sister. Slave.

But it is not to us he walks when at last he steps into the village, shining with the fire of his fasting. It is to Second Uncle's door he runs. They disappear inside my uncle's house for the evening meal without a glance at the women who wait in the entrance.

Every day will be a trial for Nanolatch now. Mornings, he will awaken before dawn and run barefoot across the sleeping village toward the cliffs. He will bathe alone, plunging down.

Brother no longer.

Gone.

WATCHING THE CLIFF

NOH

He stands, bareskinned, upon the cliffs, long before sunrise. Alone. The whitecaps toss below. Seals wail and the wind rushes between the red cliffs and the sea. His mind will whiten, empty out all thoughts. The fear. The cold. He jumps in the foggy air.

Down.

He will plunge into dark waters, his veins humming like a fish. He will dive until at last Second Uncle calls for him to come ashore. Nanolatch will kneel at his feet with his head bowed. His skin, as red as salmon flesh, will feel the raw lash of the cedar whip from his uncle's hand. Until he is both hot and cold at the same time.

Whitening. Tightening. Shivering.

Until nothing matters. The morning. The fog. The winter sea.

His uncle will hand him his garments and Nanolatch will fall into them as if they were blankets. He will gather kindling from the woods beside me to awaken the morning's fire before his uncle's family arises. There will be light and warmth in their house on dark winter mornings.

Nanolatch gleams beside the fire like a wet
seal. His chest broadens and his legs lengthen
like tree trunks. His body is as streamlined as a
muscled salmon.

He pretends he does not see Nana and me.

How I waited to tell him everything, but
silence wraps around him like storm clouds.
He did not come. All the power Grandmother
says I have is nothing beside him.

I walk in two worlds—one of day and one of
night. Easy for me to slip anywhere. No one
notices me. I am as invisible as a ghost. No
one, not even Nanolatch, dares guess what I
carry with me.

*

Nana is smooth and round at the edges, her
chest swelling softly. If only she could dive
into the sea with him each winter morning.
Hear the roar of the white waves below. The
screech of gulls above.

Leap.

Plunge down into darkness. Surface with her
lungs splitting wide open in the sea salt air.
Swim the early morning laps along the shore
with the seals. Run out with flush-red salmon
skin and a body so tingling alive, it runs heat
through her veins all day long into night.

Men become men by themselves. They need

no help from women. They go their way alone. She longs to go with her brother but she knows it is taboo. She should not even be watching him now from the door of the Big House, unseen by the sleepers. If they were brothers, she believes it would be different. She would dive beside him. Surely their totem would be so powerful that the salmon would still run strong in the rivers.

Only one can rule on land, they have both been told. He wants it more. She roams the land without finding a home. The warmth of the fire-pit does not content her as it does the other women.

She is a young girl. The tribe expects her to grow into a woman. A weaver. A wife who will sleep by another fire when she weds. A woman who will wait for the men to come home from fishing.

But she remembers something else. Remembers it dimly, as if searching for a gemstone deep in murky water.

The remembering will split her from all she knows—The Place of Mists, the tribe, and her twin brother, Nanolatch.

I will not leave her.

Where the
Salmon Leap

CHAPTER 19

Taboo

NANOLATCH

Something we must give.
Something we cannot live without.
Something dearly loved.

Drums beat slowly as we head across the sea. Heavily our paddles hit the water. The fishermen's faces hang lean and long, their lips pressed tightly together. Shilka watches in the lead, forever spilling chants. Above our heads, mocking birds clack.

We do not rest when we reach upriver. We climb straight up to the mountaintop in the dark, thirty men and twenty women strong, anointing our faces with ash. Shilka blows candlefish smoke into our

faces to hide us from the Ekas. He sings to our
ancestors, the Ravens, to save us.

I am first to spring up when the ceremony ends.
My sister rises like my shadow, running after me.
Behind us, Shilka's voice trails thinly on the wind,
calling our names.

There is only one place to go. We race to the
riverbank, falling flat on our bellies. We trail our
hands through the water and watch downstream in
the moonlight. But there is no sign. Not one fish.
The fishermen do not even bother to dip the traps. I
push myself up.

"The salmon did not hear Shilka," I sigh.

"We must call louder then," Nana insists. "We
must call from our heart."

"What magic we had is gone," I complain. "We
won't get it back by singing to a river."

My sister slams her fists flat down on the
ground. She leans over, her face close to mine.

"You are the one who's stopped calling. When
the salmon ran strong, you and I were strong. We
drew the salmon here. No one else. Now only my
voice is heard. You have abandoned us."

"All I dream about is getting things right!" I
shout. "I train all winter to become so powerful that
the salmon will return. If they do not, it is because I
have failed. I must bring them back and save the
tribe."

"You can't do it alone!" Nana yells back. "We
both must act."

The ground shakes beneath our feet. Above us, a shadow drops, making us both spin around. Shilka whirls his staff high above his shoulder, ready to slam it down on our heads.

"It is taboo for you two to be here alone!" he screeches. "Look around you. The tribe is not down from the mountains yet."

I remember how he warned us again and again never to be alone here.

I argue with the shaman. "But we are both together—"

"You are Salmon Twins. You are not like the rest of us. You are unprotected without the tribe."

"Why do we need to be protected?" I mock him. "Surely the salmon will not harm us."

"It is not the salmon who are here right now," Shilka's words echo along the riverbank. "Ekas wait for you both. Once, they stole your great-great-grandfather's soul. They will try to steal yours too."

Shilka's eyes dart in all directions. He lifts his rattle, shaking it faster and faster. Trees sway around us, touched by invisible hands.

"How can the Ekas do that?" I demand.

Shilka taps his staff on my chest. "They will grab it out of your chest and drown it right here in the river. You will die fast."

Beneath the shaman's painted face there is only weariness. He has not brought the salmon back.

"The Way is broken," he frowns. "The Way says you must give something in return for what you wish to receive. It spins the circle of death and rebirth."

What could we give? I wonder. *We have nothing left. Only hunger.*

"What magic can we use to call the salmon back?" I taunt him.

The shaman sneers. "There is no magic that will bring the salmon back. Only sacrifice. Sacrifice of something dearly loved."

Shilka's words beat a rhythm, tapping inside my head, reminding me of what Father feared at the Country Beyond the Ocean. Sacrifice—the one thing he would not allow. The words give me bait and I grab them.

"What does the tribe dearly love?"

The shaman spins around with a look so dark that Nana jumps.

"What is hardest to give up. What we believe we cannot live without."

Shilka sputters his words like a curse. His rattle shakes. Even the clamshells sewn into his tunic chatter. He bangs on the ground with his bare feet. Then he disappears into the woods where no one can talk to him.

A lone guard takes his place. Silence drops over us like a net.

Something rolls in my mind like thunder. But I whisper in Nana's ear. "The tribe has something they dearly love—a treasure—given to you."

My sister gasps. She covers her ears so she won't

hear what I hiss next.

"The totems!" Nana screams at me. "They are sacred! Carved ahead of our birth. Before anyone even knew we were coming."

The guard's eyes shift our way. I grab my sister's arm and yank her behind a fir.

"We must sacrifice them," I insist.

My sister holds her hands to her chest as if she has trouble breathing. But she stops yelling and watches me closely.

"How?" she asks.

"There is only one way to sacrifice," I tell her. My words drop over her like stones, for she covers her ears now. She knows I speak of the Way of the Dead, how a body is stretched over a fire and eaten by flames, until nothing remains but ash.

"No! It is taboo!" She steps back from me.

"You are wrong. The tribe will thank us for our sacrifice when the salmon return."

My sister's eyes pierce me like fishhooks. "You ask me to give up what is sacred to me. Why can't you sacrifice your gift instead?"

"My harpoon is a weapon that will bring food to the tribe," I tell her. "Besides, we will burn the totems together. Then the tribe will accept it."

"The tribe will condemn me!" she cries. "I am already an outcast."

"Our village believes in the ancestors. We must sacrifice the totems to release their Spirits," I insist.

"It will save the salmon. That was why our

great-great-grandfather made them for us."
I plant my feet wide apart and stare down at
Nana. I have become a thunder cloud, brooding and
dark. A million sharp lightning bolts to toss. I will
spill myself out. Until the salmon run strong, nothing will stop me.

STORM BREWING

Noh

Behind the firs, the two of them plot with their
heads together. How their words flame the air,
scorching my ears. But the girl's lips are shut.
This secret, unlike all the others, she will not
tell me. A dark worry takes root in my mind.
Nanolatch sometimes avoids me for days,
running past me by the river, so that I want to
break my vow of silence and shout his name
aloud. But then he suddenly appears. A hair-
breadth away from me he creeps so that I feel
his breath upon my cheek, warm and sweet.
He stares at me so long that the sun shifts in
the sky, and yet not one word does he speak.
And once—I shall never forget—he traced my
scar with quivering fingers. It made me shiver.
These two drift, one upstream, the other
downstream, where none can follow, not even
me. My spirit roams after them as if I were fog.

I long to attach myself to them both. But they are splitting down the middle. If they do, so must I. We are three knots on the same line. One jerk yanks us all.

All summer the fishing racks sit, empty and dry. The wind blows haunted tunes through their empty wood. Voices call from somewhere downstream.

Warnings. Whisperings.

Sorrow hangs in the fishermen's arms, empty of spears. It echoes in their heavy footsteps around the camp. Sometimes they pause to watch me as I drift past, and I hear them murmuring to one another. This one casts a shadow wherever she goes, they say. The men look to the river and back at me. The curse upon our salmon arrived with her, they all agree.

In this deep green world, nothing lives. The river runs empty. Not one salmon swims back. Not one basket will we drop at the elders' feet at the end of this season.

We all move in a dream.

Shilka cannot cure this illness. Yet everyone hangs upon him. To catch his secrets, Nanolatch slyly baits him like a fish. Nana studies him, weighing everything he says as if coppers flow from his mouth. Shilka is as empty as a rotten log. Hollow.

Their chief has no power either. His words

cut the air so I cannot breathe. No female
could flourish near him. Even his wife, who
lives in his shadow, must keep her eyes low-
ered so she does not show her pain.

My father, Fire Holder, never raised his voice.
Never would he own a slave. His words were
warm. He spun a web of safety around all the
village. He loved us. That was the fire he held.
It bound us to him. He was strong enough to
marry a shaman, my mother. When she spoke,
it was he who listened—he who followed the
Way she foretold, who gathered the villagers to
dig the herbs she needed. But even she, a bold
and clever shaman, who halted the wind and
drew our fishermen back to shore in storms,
could not stop the wind that carried the Kwakiutls in.

The Ekas fly close. I sent dreams once, wishing the twins speed at their tasks. But now
Nanolatch moves too quickly. He is on his
own.

I fear what the twins might do. Perhaps the
grandmother will stop them. Whatever spirits
the two calls, may it be the Ravens, who they
say guard this clan. Pray they do not invoke
the evil ones. For I have felt their darkening
upon my family, like a wild storm pressing
each and every one flat. None were left standing.

Place of Mists

CHAPTER 20

Moon of the Popping Trees

Midwinter

NANA

Winter snaps the young and old. In the dark days,
the dim time, it grabs them. When ice coats the tree
branches it happens. If you walk beneath them, you
can hear the branches crack, a dying song. It is
Grandmother who breaks this winter. We carry her
body to the burial grounds and lay it upon wooden
racks, flat to the sky. Snowflakes fall and melt upon
her gray hair. The wrinkles on her face are smooth,
as if she spins for eternity a blanket of sky. But her
body is thin and brittle, shrunken to the bone.

Father lights the burial fire beneath her. Flames
leap higher and higher until they cover what was
once my grandmother. The wind sweeps her ashes

out to sea, spreading our memories of her all over
the winter village.

She is flying, flying everywhere, at such a speed.
Seeing everything in fullness that was only a shadow before. Her cloak brushes me with sharp frozen
edges, hard and icy against my flesh. Each touch is a
remembrance. A wound. A word.

It is my job to watch over the burial site. I bring
mussels sweetened with cranberries and crunchy
seaweed, her favorites. Each morning, I fill baskets
with spring water in case she should feel thirst on
her wanderings. I talk to her. As long as we talk to
the Dead, she taught me, they remain with us.

I raise my hand to the sky to catch a piece of her
flying ash and close my fist on nothing. She is flying
everywhere. I cannot contain her.

Nanolatch does not join me at Grandmother's
resting place. He watches from a distance. Fog swirls
between us, yet I feel his dark brown eyes upon me,
glistening.

The women call my name through the mist.
Na-na! Na-na! My name rolls endlessly along the
shoreline. The fishwives think I have sat, dreaming,
at Grandmother's funeral fire long enough. Her fire
is cold. Ashless. Snowflakes swirl around my head.
The damp air bites through me as if I am naked.
Even my friend Noh is miles away at her chores,
absorbed. She shakes her head at Nanolatch whenever he walks too close to me.

When I enter the plankhouse, I bend over to fit

through the raven's mouth carved in the bottom of
the totem pole. I remember Grandmother stooping
low, squeezing her body inside. How we dove in
front of her, giggling and shouting in her ears. How
she laughed, reaching out with her warm hands
through the dimness veiling her sight.

All eyes follow me as I join the fishwives at the
fire. Grandmother's spot is empty. I sit at the right
of it still. This winter I will weave my first blanket
from a pattern Father drew. It shows our village, the
long plankhouses, side by side, with their doors facing the sea.

I will take the blanket with me when I wed,
Mother says. My mother once was taken from the
Nootkas, her family, to wed my father. She brought
all her blankets with her as wedding gifts.

"So frightened was I to cross the sea, and seasick
too, that I kept my eyes on my weaving the whole
trip," she tells me. "Your father ordered my blankets
to be hung at once on the walls of the Big House so I
could always see them."

I saw my mother greet her Nootka relatives at
the betrothal ceremony, tears in her eyes. "Sister!"
she cried. "Nephew!" she marveled. They only visit
here once in awhile. When they depart across the
sea, she is silent for many days. If once she protested
leaving her home, my mother has forgotten it now. I
too am expected to sleep at another fire-pit a long
distance from here. Take nothing of my life with me
except a weaving.

"This black is for the border. It will toss like waves at sea when you look at the blanket," Mother says. "You will weave layer upon layer of these two summer wools to make the houses stand out from shore."

The plankhouses are the color of the tall grasses at the end of summer, a parched brown spun with flecks of buttercup yellow. My hands tug at the wool but they do not dance. The delicate thread snaps in two. After weeks of weaving, my frowning mother yanks out all my threads. I must begin again. The fishwives lean their heads together and whisper. The blanket will not be finished before winter's end. My new husband will not be pleased.

My sigh is like the wind whipping in from the winter sea.

CHAPTER 21

Spirits Releasing

NANOLATCH

I pace the shore every evening. My desires are arrows flung to the wind. I am churned up, a storm crouched at the edge of the beach, waiting, slate gray.

One night, my sister steps out of the burial grounds. Alone. Since Grandmother's leavetaking, we have not spoken.

"Salmonwife!" I call her.

She is about to run when she sees me, but the word stops her dead. No one ever calls her that name. I am at her side in an instant. Her face looks stunned, as if someone has grabbed her. Her eyes shift in all directions, fearful of what the spirits might do.

"Have you thought over our plan?" I ask.

The icy wind whips around us, blasting our words every which way. We draw our cedar capes tight. She stares at me but does not speak.

"We have lost the salmon and Grandmother too. This winter, more elders could die," I urge her. "We will work harder for our food. There is no time for any ceremonies, only time for work. The curse lingers. We must do something."

I hear her voice, thin and wavering in the wind. "We are children. This is not our work. It is for the elders to decide."

"You don't believe that. We are Salmon Twins— sent to save this tribe. You told me so yourself. No one, even our father and Shilka, can do what must be done."

"We cannot break the spell," Nana looks toward the Salmon House, dim and quiet, out at sea.

"Tonight, when everyone is asleep," I insist, "meet me in the Ceremonial House!"

I run off and leave her standing there before she can answer. As I pass the totem poles, a shadow leans out, watching. I spin around. It disappears like smoke.

That night I wait at the doorway of my family's plankhouse. The light from the fire dims. One by one, my father and my mother and the michimis say goodnight and stretch out on their sleeping mats. The heaviness of their breathing soon fills the room.

I tiptoe inside. Nana tosses restlessly and stares up
at the roof. My stomach tightens into a hard fist. I
step toward the fire and sink a rope into it until it
catches flame. I hold it within my cupped palm and
creep outside, yanking my sister's sleeve as I go. She
looks up but does not budge.

Inside the Ceremonial House, a hush hides in
the corners like whispers. Only sea breath and dust
roll on the floor. No celebrations here. A dry bone
year. Just laying out of the Dead.

I set kindling into the fire-pit and drop my rope
into it. Fire soon sparks in the dim room. Nearby I
find the ancient totems waiting side by side.
Footsteps scuff the ground.

"Nana?"

There is no answer. Just an eeriness in the room.
I stare into each dark corner. Nothing.

Finally my sister appears in the doorway. I rise
to greet her. But just as I reach her, a figure steps out
of the shadows. Noh rushes between us, her black
hair flying.

"Don't do this!" she spreads her hands wildly.

Noh's voice creaks, full of rust. She who has
been silent not only talks but also speaks our own
language and knows our plans. She could betray us
in an instant.

"Who taught you to speak?" Nana gasps.

Noh points to us both.

"Not me!" I protest. "I spoke to Noh at times and
she listened. None of us guessed how clever she is."

Nana shakes her head. "I spoke to you but you never spoke back. I thought my secrets were safe with you. You always seemed to read my thoughts."

Noh nods. "I am my mother's daughter. She taught me to watch and listen carefully. To learn another's language. Then I would know all. Find why I was sent here. I come to save you, Nana."

I pull my sister's arm. "We don't have much time. The fire will die down soon. We must act now."

But Noh grabs Nana's other arm. How often have I felt the three of us, each one separate, yet somehow moving together, branches of the same tree. Now we are one long line, a tree in a windstorm, yanked in all directions.

"You will be sorry!" warns Noh. "The two of you are one. This will split you apart forever."

I free my sister from Noh's grasp and drag her to the fire-pit. Nana looks back, her eyes on Noh.

"Please, Nana!" Noh calls out.

My sister stares back and forth from Noh to me, her eyes red.

By then smoke clouds the room, so I stir the sticks up again. I clutch the male totem and set the other one in my sister's hands.

"You are Salmonwife. You are the only one who can burn your totem. Will you sacrifice it for the tribe?"

Noh squats, shaking her head. She looks ready to plead with my sister again.

"This is our doing," I tell her firmly. "Not yours."

Noh sinks back on her heels, wrapping her arms tightly around her body. She rocks back and forth and does not say another word.

I drop my totem into the flame. Nana strokes her totem doll longingly then lifts it high above the fire-pit. She lets it fall. Noh cries out. The cedar totems reach their arms up to dive into another world. They darken, then crack into pieces. We stare as the cedar turns to ash. I pour water over the fire and spread the ashes flat.

"We will know soon if it worked," I whisper to Nana.

It is deep dark outside. My sister and Noh creep back into the Big House separately. But I crouch in the doorway, hidden inside the raven's mouth. Tonight I will stay close and not return to my own mat. I must keep watch. Something might happen at anytime.

In the still room, Noh takes her place by my sister's mat. Her eyes light up the dark like flames. All night long, I look into them and see the totems burning.

CHAPTER 22

Nothing But Ash

NANA

Someone shakes me awake. It is full light. The air is shocked with loud chants, ancient words that I do not understand. Shaman's spells I wish to hide from. I bolt upright. Both my parents squat before me. My mother's robe is wet with tears. Her hair is undone, spilling out of its braid. Father's face is streaked with ash. Nanolatch stands beside them, his hands bound behind his back.

I want to close my eyes and forget. But I remember my totem lifting her arms up higher and higher, leaping into the flame out of my hands. Her flat body etched in fish scales. Nothing I could do to stop her.

Gone.

Just a cedar branch burning.

The chanting stops. Shilka steps forward, striking the sand with his staff.

"I smell something shameful! The wind carries the scent of burning cedar. Ancestor's ashes. And a voice. Your great-great-grandfather cries out from the burial grounds. A fire eats his soul. His totems have burned."

Shilka opens his hand. Dove gray ash smolders in his bare palm. He throws his head back and screeches. His cries echo along the shoreline like the mourning cries of Grandmother after First Uncle died.

"Why have you done this, child?" Father's eyes are heat red. He points straight at me.

A million reasons never to be told. The two of us with the same face, called to act, not knowing how to unleash the spirits. I did not want to lose my brother forever. I saw him slipping away from me, journeying downstream into waters I could not swim, where the salmon roamed out of my grasp. So I dove in after him.

Besides, Father, I could not go to you. You were gone from me.

"She has not done this," my brother shouts, his voice full of lightning sparks. "She tried to stop me. I lit the flame. It was my decision to make this sacrifice so the salmon would run again."

Shilka makes rumbling sounds in his throat. He

looks ready to explode.

"It is taboo to harm a totem," Father's face darkens, as if he were aflame.

"Is it taboo to try to save the tribe?" Nanolatch's eyes blaze. "If no one else does anything in this village, then I must."

My father slams his fist against the tall totem poles that hold up the dwelling. All around us, the Big House trembles on its legs. My mother steps back, as if she could disappear into the walls. I listen for the wind rushing by, a sign of Grandmother's Spirit flying near. But she is not here to shelter me anymore.

"It does not matter who lit the flame," Father says. "The totems were Nana's and they were destroyed. You will both be punished."

"Don't punish Nana!" Nanolatch begs. "She only wished to save us. If I cannot defeat the curse, she is our only hope. Spare her."

The heat of my brother's words touches me with the same warmth of Grandmother's hands. Soft. Familiar. My tears drip like endless coastal rain. My brother is so near in this room, yet as far away as downstream. In a corner, Noh rocks back and forth, crying.

"Enough!" Father roars. "You, Nanolatch will not speak to your sister until spring, when she is wed. You will not eat any flesh this winter. And you, Nana, will not leave this house. You will spend the entire winter weaving. You will not be allowed out until your Initiation."

A scream struggles to rise out of my throat, where all my lost words are trapped. They burn in a heap, unspoken, in that dark place.

The features of my face flatten out. My body cracks.

I am a cedar branch burning.

LISTENING GIRL

NOH

Outside, the coastal rain falls, endless and dreary. She stays inside. Dyed wool dangles from the walls, swaying back and forth, drying all this long winter. These are the strands that once she and her grandmother combed and gathered.

It seems long ago. She does not remember it now.

She weaves wool into the blanket, squinting in the dim light. She does not follow the pattern laid out for her by her father. She draws the wool in and out, choosing only a boiled, dirty white. She weaves a blank sameness into the cloth.

Her mind drifts.

She longs to dive deep, swim out to sea with her grandmother who is flying everywhere. But

there is only rain and fog, and she cannot go.
Cannot fill the burial sacks with water or
gather crisp seaweed for the ghosts to crunch.
She weaves beside the fishwives, who huddle
around the winter fire, gossiping, growing fat
on their bones. They nod their heads together
and whisper about her. Punishment, they
agree. It must be done.

She longs to hear her brother's voice. She has
not spoken to him for many moons or even
caught a glimpse of him. She remembers how
his words sounded when last he spoke, how his
words danced softly to protect her.

She listens for him along the shoreline where
he lands the sea's catch. She listens to the
other voices toss on the wind. High and bold,
they call to her, the voices of her Salmon
Brothers, stirring.

She finally lifts her head to listen.

CHAPTER 23

Wild Goose Moon

NANA

When they squawk, I know they call for me. Geese honk from far off, long before you see them. You can stand still and wait for them to fly overhead or you can face south. They always fly from there when the weather changes, heat at their backs, the cool north ahead of them. They yell out to one another to keep flying, stay in line, leader at the head, into darkness.

In the spring of their fourteenth year, Kwakiutl girls journey high to the cliffs hanging above the sea, resting on a wide ledge, below the highest cliff top. They paint red ochre on their faces and fast seven days and seven nights. There they wait from one new moon until the next. Afterward, they climb down to bathe in the sea. The children they once were swim behind them like a long-lost memory. When they walk out of the waves they are forever changed.

Shilka wraps me so tightly in bark that I cannot take a full breath. Round and round, the straps press me in. Shreds of goat hair are tucked between, covering my nakedness. The fur will keep me warm without a fire for the long days alone ahead of me. A strand of my hair is sliced off. My eyebrows are plucked one by one.

Pieces of me falling off. Never to be the same girl again.

Mother cries but lifts her head high. Father, at her side, nods his head. In the distance Noh stands like a wooden totem. My brother halts on the sand, a silent figure, watching me walk away.

I cannot climb the cliff, swinging up as usual. Instead, I walk the long path around in my bare feet with my arms bound flat against my sides. Not one mouthful of food, or even a water sack, has been offered. It takes all afternoon to reach the caves. No one is there to greet me. There is no soft mat to lie upon.

I believed all my life Grandmother would guide me where I most feared to go. She would make certain I am safe. Not like Girl Who Is Gone, who jumped at her own shadow afterward. Grandmother was the only one who would have had the right to accompany me here. She knew long ago that her time was short. She urged me on. And I was so unwilling to learn.

I remember her stories of my great-great-grandfather carving the Twin Salmon totems in the dark of winter. During his elder years, how he must have longed to see Nanolatch and me swim past him. But he did not live to see our birth. I never saw his face. I burned his totem. I didn't learn Grandmother's lessons in time.

To my Initiation I come empty-handed. Shameful, the fishwives muttered all winter, their whispers hissing around the fire-pit.

Everyone abandons me. Even the spirits.

From the ledge on the cliffs, in my old hiding spot, I look down at the distance between the village and me. My tears fall. I, who always climbed away from the tribe, am forever separate. I howl so loudly the fishermen stop in the sand and turn their heads upward. Away from the edge I crawl, far from them. There is no guide to help me. I must do this in my own way, the way I have done everything else.

Apart.

For days I doze on and off. Each time, awakening with my eyes flying open. Studying the tree branches and grasses for movement. Listening for the footsteps of the Spirits moving closer, evil ones approaching. Again, I sleep.

After many days, I lose track of the time. I know no hunger. My body feels light, almost as if it is not here anymore. My mind looks down at me. In and

out, my Spirit roams like mist. The world is alive. I
can hear it breathe. Twigs crackle. Branches sway
behind me as if to warn me.

Footsteps sink heavily into the ground.

They have come, whoever they are, to battle
over me. What I do now will determine my whole
life ahead of me. It will hang on the thread of these
days. Look and be turned into stone like a Spiritless
One. Run and then hide forever.

Be still, orders the voice.

I sit straight up and close my eyes. Make my
back a plank of wood. But the footsteps press closer.
Branches creak against one another, crying out
warnings. The wind lifts. Something taps me with a
million sharp pricks. Hard, wet scales beat against
my skin. I squeeze my body into a tight ball. My
heart roars like a waterfall.

Remember.

I don't know if I can. I forget how to do it. Tears
choke my throat.

Breathe. Watch the breaths.

My breaths are gasps I cannot catch hold of. Like
storm waves, they toss in fury. Hot breath blows on
my bare shoulder. Cold claws tighten around my
neck. Fire blackens the air.

A gust of spring wind blows fresh and cool, loud
with the calls of passing geese. I pull hard and long
on my lungs, filling myself with coolness as I
breathe in, pushing the fear out as I exhale. Everything is suspended. No more footsteps. No more

sharp points like needles against my face. The thing
that had grabbed me lightly brushes me now.

Hold fast!

I do not think. I am no longer me. Just breath—
riding in and out. Sun touches my hair and I know
warmth. Later, dampness spills everywhere. Dew
rises up from the ground. It turns into night, then
day, then night again. Second day or seventh day, I
do not remember. The smell of smoke burns the air.

Salmonwife!

Who calls me by that name?

One who knows you well.

I hold my breath. A woman's voice. Sharp as a
seagull's cry. A figure swirls in front of me. Not
Dzonowka.

Grandmother!

I see her with my eyes shut. She is smiling,
dressed in a white robe.

*You must go from here. Seek your Way. It opens
before you now.*

Where is it?

*You will find it Where the Salmon Leap. You
must rise and take the journey there without the
tribe. You are the One the salmon await. You have
passed the test.*

What test?

*The Initiation. You have pushed past your fear.
Now you will find out who you really are.*

Who is that?

You are Salmonwife. Meant to wed the Salmon

*Men. Not meant to wed any human. You will save
the tribe if you do this.*
What must I do?
*Open your eyes now! See what has happened to
all your fear.*
My eyelids still press down heavily, not wanting
to see.
It is safe, child.
I take a deep breath and peek. In front of me, the
great monster Sisiutl spins in a circle of fire and
smoke, its tendrils scorching. It screams, swirling in
a spiral like a long tunnel. Twirling like a black
whirlwind to the very edge of the cliff. It heaves
itself down into the sea.
I turn around to thank her, but Grandmother is
nowhere to be seen. Only the tree branches swirl.
One last word I hear from her.
Go!

THE ONES WHO JOURNEY WITH ME

NOH

Drumming. Deep drumming.
I think it beats inside me. I think at first that
it is my heart.
On the horizon, lights flash far out at sea.
Blankets of light shimmer, like a dance you

sometimes see on winter nights. Yellow bright with sparks of red.

But it is a spring morning. Michimis gather mussels by the beach and slaves carry water baskets. No one stops at their tasks. Soon the taises will awaken, and they alone might be able to see it.

Something is happening to the world. No one must know, except us three—Nana, Nanolatch, and me.

I must hide this light from the Kwakiutls. One lived who could have taught me that— Wind Tamer. She spoke to the wind as if it were alive. That was her power. She had faith it would move just as she wanted, and it did. She flung her arms in all the directions of the wind—whirling them, stirring the air—until the wind rushed around her.

My feet run off before me, down to the beach.

There is a powerful place on shore, by the edge of the bay where the land turns south. I have always longed to stand there.

Grandmother knew it well. I remember her lifting her arms to the water to call the spirits. The sea splashed at her feet. Fish swam in the current right toward her, spinning on their tails to witness her strength.

I stand like she once did, my arms lifted high. My legs quiver beneath me, and my breath catches in my throat. I close my eyes and tell the wind to come. Ravens caw in my ears, so close that their sharp wingtips slice through my hair. And then, faintly, the wind shifts. Wet and warm, it blows from the south. I feel a shadow pass by as clouds cover the sky. Waves crash loudly. Fog rolls in. Raindrops spit at my face. When I open my eyes, the sea is hidden behind clouds.

A darkening shape rolls toward me, purple within the snow-white fog. Something inside me opens up wide. I hear all the worlds speaking, all the voices of the ones who travel with me.

Then one voice comes.

We await you. From our village, we cry out to you. You were taken from us and long have we mourned. But you had a task to accomplish first before we could find you again.

Mother!

We live, daughter. All our warriors are buried, but we are safe. Your aunts and elders. Dancing Bear. Gift From the Clouds. Red Cod Running.

Long have I waited for you, Mother. In dreams. In thought. But you never came.

There were tests for you to pass first. You are ready now. I am your guardian spirit. Such a thing the mother of a shaman can be. I will send you all my strength, although it may be my last. Go to your task!

As quickly as she has come, Wind Tamer
blows away. I twirl where all can see me. I spin
away the years of slavery, as if it were just a
winter cape I once wore. My family awaits me.

The girl awaits me too. Her journey is not
over. There is one other I need to call now.
With my mother's help, I can do it.

I have a charm to make her brother come to
me this time. Once before, I called to him in
the fishermen's language. But he would not follow despite his promise. His fear was greater
than his love, I think. That dawn, after the ceremonies, I already sensed it. If he won't come, I
told myself, then I will take a piece of him
with me. Off I snipped the tips of his hair with
my knife blade, so softly that he did not stir. It
has taken me a while to weave it into a charm.
One part is his hair. Another, dried snakeskin.
The last part is the skin of a toad. All are tied
in a bundle at my waist. It is my grandmother's
potion, the one that bound my grandfather to
her side forever.

In a circle, round and round I spin, grasping
the bundle, whispering his name.

"Nanolatch! Come here to me!"

The rain pours down. The beach is empty. I
keep spinning. At my back, I hear footsteps.
Before I turn, I know who it is. His face is
whirling. He comes to tell me what I already
know.

"Your family lives, Noh," he cries out. "I cannot keep it secret any longer. All the women and children in your village wait."

Nanolatch steps toward me. My arms open wide and I shut my eyes. His arms wrap around my body so closely that I no longer feel I am in this world anymore. We are no longer two. We are one.

He lets me go a little before he leans down to kiss me. Not on the forehead, where my father did, but on my lips where I have never felt a kiss before. At first, it burns like forest fire. Then it lifts me up as if I had wings. I feel I can do anything, even fly back to my family— such is the power of his kiss.

"You are the one I have watched from afar," I tell him, "always longing for you."

"You are the one I love," he confesses. "From the first moment I saw you, I felt I had known you always. My spirit was not whole until you came."

Each glance from this man makes me more solid. Although I drift far from home, I plant my feet on Kwakiutl sand and grow as I was meant to, because of him. I let his words roll through me, adding fire to the joy of my mother's return. I am so lit up, I feel like a beacon of light.

But I cannot savor it long.

"Did you see the horizon this morning, Nanolatch?"

He smiles. "So bright it awoke me. Though none stirred in the plankhouses, it was like sunshine calling me outside to find you."

"The light shines because there is a change in the world—the one we wait for. We must act. We cannot do it without your sister. I must win her to our side. Long have you left her alone."

"She goes her own way," he shrugs. "Soon she will wed the Nootka boy and leave this village. How can we stop it?"

I look up to the cliffs. Nothing moves there. A shiver blows through me. "I must go to her now before it is too late. Do not follow me. Wait for me here!"

One last lingering kiss he gives me, begging me to stay longer with him. But the drumming returns, beating inside my ears, so I no longer hear his words of love calling me back.

Off I run with a speeding heart.

CHAPTER 24

Coming into Light

NANA

Set on the ground are my favorite spring treats. Fried
eulachon and smelts. Stewed salmonberries. Roasted
clams. Big fistfuls I cram into my mouth but immediately spit them out. They are cold and moldy.
Time must have passed. Someone brought food to
break my fast and left my white garment too. Who
came and went, I do not know. I have been somewhere else, with my eyes shut tight. Yet I have not
moved from this spot on the cliff.

My body returns from where it was flying. With
those few bites, it sinks back down into me. I feel
newly born. The years I've lived here by the sea
seem like a dream.

I become her now—Salmonwife.

Out I push my arms from their bindings—layers of cedar bark and goat hair. Shaking my head, I loosen my dark hair from its braid until it falls around me like an animal's mane. I step into the white robe. I find myself dancing, laughing, and pounding my feet down hard as if at potlatch. Lifting my arms up to the skies as I remember Grandmother doing. Rejoicing. I imagine I hear music from far off.

And then I feel them.

Out at sea they are stirring. Singing along with me. Spinning on their tails. Stretching their gills wide open. I tiptoe to the very edge of the cliff where the ledge hangs out. Then I shrink back. Light shines so brightly from the Salmon House that I fear everyone below will see it too. It is as if a thousand eulachon burn end to end there.

Grandmother's words come, so clear that it's as if she just sang them.

You will be filled with light.
No darkness will dim it.
The Way will be certain.
There will be no doubt.

Later that day, Noh lifts herself over the cliff, the sun a red ball at her back. She sets a basket down in front of me. She opens her mouth to speak but grows still when she sees my face. We are like two shining seas staring at one another. I wonder if she has changed. Or is it just I?

She is lit up brightly like the sun upriver. She seems to have floated up to this mountaintop. All her ash is cleansed away. A streak of red ochre covers her scar, announcing unknown joys. Her hair is soft and shiny. Gone is her flat mask. She smiles for the first time, making her look more beautiful than my own mother.

"What has happened, Noh?"

"My family still lives," she spills the words out. "Your father spared them, Nana."

My heart lifts with her words. *Do not kill the innocents!* It was what I pleaded silently at that long-ago tribal gathering. My father must have heard it somehow, though he gave no sign.

"How do you know this is true?"

"Your brother told me before he kissed me."

"I should have guessed how he felt. So often I saw him watching you. But how does he know such things?"

"He heard it from his uncle. He wanted me to know the truth because he loves me."

"What will you do, now that you know?"

"So much is happening. I have to wait and see what it all means. I came by here on the eighth day to bring food. You did not stir so I left you with your spirits. I watched the cliff every day for movement but did not see you. Shilka forbade me to visit."

"How many days have I not been here?" I gasp.

Noh twists her head. "Why, you have been here many days—from new moon to full moon. One day short of the next new moon. This morning I saw the light on the sea, and I sensed all the fish stirring as if they were reborn. That's why I climbed up."

"Then all the tribe will know!"

She shakes her head. "They do not have eyes to see as we do. We were bound since our birth to the Spirit World. We have always sensed such things. They do not."

"And my brother?"

Noh pauses. "He sees it too but keeps things to himself. You must tell me your plan, now that the salmon have stirred."

"Why do you think I have a plan?" I step back from her. "The tribe expects me to come down soon."

"You are not the girl we knew before. Now you are wondrous. Wild and free. Besides, the Nootka boy has arrived, shouting orders at the fishwives for how his marriage stew must be prepared. You will hate him. Tell me what you will do. I can help you."

When I first met Noh, I named her after my childhood friend, the one who knew all my secrets. Somehow, she has become that friend. My brother loves and trusts her now. He would tell her the truth.

"I am going upriver," I confess. "Don't tell me not to go. I must."

Noh shakes her head. "You should not go there

alone! We must find a way to protect you."

I fold my arms across my chest.

"I have been right before," she insists. "Burning the totems only made trouble for you. Let us both wait and think how to do it right."

"My spirit guide told me to go now."

"Stay just this one night," she begs. "Rest here until morning. Wait!"

She runs to the cliff and scurries down instead of taking the path. There is no use arguing with Noh. She seems to know everything. I peek into the basket she left. Baked herring in its own rich oil—still hot—and fish stew. I fill my belly then lean against a tree, yawning.

But then I remember that the tribe will expect me to have finished my task. Someone may come to check on me soon. Already the day is ending. The sun will touch the water and be swallowed by it. If I sleep now, when I awaken there will be no choice but to go down to the Ceremonial House where the Nootkas await.

Noh is wrong. The burning of the totems started something. It broke through the barrier that separated the Spirits from me. They saw that I was willing to do anything, even what is taboo. I must listen to them now. They will come to help.

All my life I knew only what I did not want. But no longer.

I am balanced on a knife's edge, looking over at each side. One, the side of tradition—the winter village, the known. The other way—upriver, where there is danger and no clear path. But to stay here, perching on this edge, is to remain the child I no longer wish to be. I scramble to my feet.

I have Grandmother's words. My spirit guide has spoken.

Go!

Above my head, the cliff edge hangs over the open sea. No girl has scaled it before. You can never look down from there—to do that would be death. It leads to sacred paths the ancient warriors once took upriver. It was the only way there if you traveled by foot. I reach up and clasp a handhold carved into the rock. Above my head is blue sky. Up and up I climb. At the top, I stretch out on flat ground, my heart drumming in my chest. It is long minutes before I can breathe.

Ahead of me is the old trail. It gleams in the twilight. But before I take a step toward it, the cliff beneath my feet trembles. Someone is climbing up.

Faster than I can run away.

CHAPTER 25

Sun Falling Down

NANA

I see his dark eyes first as he draws himself level with me. He crawls, straight and soundless, toward me. He pushes me down flat so no one can see us from below.

"It is taboo to visit a girl on her fasting trial!" I yell.

"You have finished your trial. Besides, your fast is broken," Nanolatch adds. "Noh told me. Where are you going?"

I have not seen my brother for many moons. He looks more like a man than my twin. The last sun-rays light his bare chest, as broad and muscled as my father's.

My lips are sealed, tight as stone. I worried that when Noh left so swiftly, she ran directly to him. What did she tell him?

"Salmonwife, tell me your plans. You have Shilka's warnings if you go alone upriver."

His voice is as soft as spring air. He has that special look he had when we used to lay belly-down by the river and the salmon ran beneath our fingers. I know his face better than my own.

"There is something I must do there. It is my home," I say. "I do not know what awaits me there, but I must go without the tribe."

"Your home is here by the sea—"

"It's your home, not mine. You will be a leader in a land of warriors. I cannot be like you. I come from the underworld. My Salmon Brothers will die, and so will our tribe if I don't return upriver. The salmon called out to us there. But you did not listen."

My brother's chest caves in. He suddenly looks small and cold, like a clam huddled in its shell.

"I have tried to save the tribe," he cries. "Even the sacrifice did not work because it was my doing. But, if we go together...you always told me the salmon run strong when you and I call them."

It is too late to return to our childhood. At this moment, the sun is swallowed blood red by the sea. Soon it will be dark.

I turn away.

My brother's arms encircle me.

"No!" I scream. "I must face the Ekas alone!"

"We will meet the Ekas together. It is taboo for you to travel to the river without the tribe. But I am just like you, from the underworld, a Salmon Twin. Together we will be safe."

He rests his hand upon my shoulder, his warmth sinking deep down through my chilled flesh.

"It is enough that you have come here," I tell him. "I will always remember that you returned to me when I thought I had lost you."

My brother grips my shoulders. "It is not enough for me! I can't let you go alone. For the rest of my life, I will wait for you to return. I would beat myself for not going with you."

He towers above me like the cliff.

"You think Noh betrayed you," he argues. "She didn't. She sent me to go with you. The tribe will search for you tomorrow if you do not climb down. They will find you easily if you walk. But you and I will go by canoe. Even if they follow us, we will get there before them."

I stare at my brother. He looks like the chief he will one day become.

If I get there before the tribe, I can do what I must do. Run the life-death journey upstream. Run by my brother's strength.

"Tonight," he orders, "meet me at the canoes when the moon rides straight above your head. We will steer by its light."

He does not wait for my answer. He crawls back

to the cliff and edges down, feet first. For one long breath, he holds still, groping the rocks for footholds beneath him. I hang over the edge, fearful that he will fall miles down into the sea. His round, brown eyes fill his dark face—my own eyes staring back at me. Quickly he descends, his long black hair trailing behind him in the twilight.

CHAPTER 26

Running
Toward You

NANA

The moon rises and arcs slowly across the sky. But I am gone long before that, creeping down the path to the edge of the village where everyone sleeps. Here and there, I stop. My legs feel weak. They wobble from fasting and sitting so long.

I wait by the canoes. The moon hangs exactly above my head, brightly watching. Up and down the sand I pace, wringing my hands. From the woods, wolves howl a lonely song. Bats flurry above me. If my brother does not come, I tell myself, I will run alone through darkness to the mountains. I will scream all the way, scaring the Ekas from my path.

Footsteps. My brother and Noh arrive. They carry food baskets, his harpoon, and cedar capes for traveling.

"Noh will go home," Nanolatch announces. "She will follow the coast at night, on foot. Hide by day. No one will guess she's gone south, for they will follow us instead. She should reach Salish land in two moons."

It hurts me to breathe when I hear it. Leaving stabs its needle through each of us. We will all depart from here and never see one another again. We must follow our own way separately. Yet Noh clings to my brother's side, pressing her thinness into him.

"You will never be anything more than a slave if you stay here," Nanolatch coaxes Noh.

"I can't stay here either," I tell her. "I want to be more than a Nootka wife."

"I...will miss you both," she murmurs. "We are linked."

"We will always be as one," my brother says. "But I cannot bear to see you live your life in shadow. Without your family. Without a destiny. If you stay, I have to ignore you. Until I am chief, I have no power to save you."

I turn to my brother. "What will you do when you are chief?"

"I will not be like Father. No slaves. No lightning raids. No tribal wars. I hope to see Noh someday. Not as conqueror. As a friend."

Noh steps back from us, letting go of my brother's hand.

"I will live with my tribe as a shaman, as I was meant to do. Sing your praise to the Salish. Tell them how you gave me freedom and that you will make the coast safe. They will bless you."

Nanolatch hangs his head.

"How can they bless a tribe that has killed so many of their own?"

The question whirls in the air among us. It snaps our mouths shut, stealing our breath away.

Noh breaks the silence. "You were not the one who killed, Nanolatch. I believe you will not harm us in the future either. I have your promise. We will change things. Between you and I, we will bring peace to the coast."

I grab the food sacks from my brother and hand them to her. "Take these. We don't need them. Salmon fast on their way upstream."

The moon begins to sink down in the sky. Noh looks up.

"Go now! Hurry!" she calls. "I will wait for you, Nanolatch."

One last touch of my brother's hand and then she twirls into the night. A rustle of her hair flies behind her like raven wings. Into the night she runs alone.

The way is long. I shudder. Anyone could find her and keep her a slave forever. My brother should go with her, not me, to keep her safe. Nanolatch watches her go, leaning into the wind she stirred. A part of him will forever follow her. Slowly he turns away. He must not think of her now. He edges down to the waiting canoes.

"We must move swiftly," he tells me. "Tomorrow morning the men will fish in the sea and notice even one small canoe missing. When you and Noh do not return, they will call Shilka to sniff our trail. He will guess where we have gone. You will have to push as fast as I do."

He hands me a smooth wooden paddle, so worn that it fits into the palm of my hand. Hands, useless at weaving, glide the carved wood firmly through the water.

We canoe that night by the light of the moon. My breath pulls in short puffs. My whole body quivers. My arms become heavy weights.

My brother says, "Sleep. I will wake you when I need you."

I sink down in a heap. Cover myself with the cedar robe, warm and snug. Water sprays above my head but I am sheltered. My body rocks back and forth. Behind me, my brother leans, sweeping the sea with his paddle like a dancer. I shut my eyes and drift. My brother carries us forward.

It grows lighter. Gray shifting to white. Dawn. My eyes flicker and I think how, just now, the fishermen will be standing by the canoes and know something is wrong. They will make a plan. I rise and look down the coast for the tribe. I imagine the fishermen—twelve canoes strong—riding in a straight line close behind us. Beating the current fast. Shilka standing in the bow, shouting orders. His fierce black face, his nose sniffing our scent on the air.

Nanolatch knows in an instant that I am awake. He yells orders—to paddle right, then left, to lean our bodies one way, then another. His eyes do not budge from the water.

"Push faster!" my brother calls out. "They will guess where we have gone by now. They will ride doublespeed to stop us. Hurry!"

It is a crisp, bright morning, full of sunbeams. Light gleams on my brother's long hair, making it glimmer like wet shale. I lean my body forward and dip my paddle deep. Push the sea behind us. We ride as one person, our paddles hitting the water together with one smooth stroke, never stopping.

When we reach the river, it is swollen with rain. Rapids. Wildness. Too early in the season for traveling through it. Fishermen have been drowned in its current in the past if they entered at this time. Our canoe bounces up and down. We are a lightweight in the current's hand. It twists in all directions then wedges us flat against shore. We push off hard.

On and on. Upward.

It is then I remember my other brothers. I call out to them above the river's roar.

Salmon Beings, we are running toward you.
Salmon Beings, we are coming closer to you.
Let me not fall asleep.
Let me not fall asleep.
Until I find you.

Where the
Salmon Leap

CHAPTER 27

Dreamspell

NANA

The sun, which journeyed with us like a bright eye, suddenly disappears. Clouds float through the sky and smother its light one by one. Yet, above the rush of the current—above the pounding of our hearts and the whipping of wind—we know we are there.

The waterfall sings out. We are home.

We drag the canoe out of the river and tiptoe along the bank. Everything waits in stillness. The dark mountains. The hidden trails. The place seems to hold its breath.

My brother must wonder why I have insisted on coming here. Yet he rode without stopping, without questions. Now he turns to me as we huddle in our cedar capes. His dark eyes search mine.

"I thought I would know when I stepped foot here what I would do," I confess to him. "But I don't know yet."

"We made it here, Nana. We rode on the river alone, and the Ekas weren't waiting to harm us. Shilka was wrong. Our totem is stronger."

Behind his head I imagine I see a shifting, a blur. But I do not say anything. I lower my eyes, calm myself, and then look up again.

A mist spills down from the mountains like steamy breath. It gathers speed as it falls, rolling over the land. A ghost blanket. It smothers everything I had seen clearly a moment before. Boulders. A tall cedar tree. The riverbank.

And then it swallows up my brother.

He cries out, "Where are you, Nana?"

"Here!" I reach my hand out but cannot find him.

The fog is so thick I cannot see my own body. I beg Nanolatch to keep talking so I will know where he is. He had just been beside me but now I cannot tell in which direction he stands. At last I touch his cold hand and hold on tight.

"The Ekas swarm around us!" I scream. "All my life they have followed me, casting spells so I could not be who I was meant to be."

"It is just mountain mist," he says.

"I have never seen a mist like this one," I tell him.

He has no answer for me. We press close, sitting back-to-back. We rock back and forth to heat ourselves. Dampness penetrates our capes. My body rattles like a sack of bones.

I try to remember why I am here. I have something to do, I am sure. But my thoughts slide, thick and slow, as if I have a head of sand. My arms feel like two tree stumps heavy with the weight of paddling. My eyelids droop. Behind me, my brother yawns and his body slumps against mine.

"Keep talking, Nanolatch! Stay awake!"

My brother does not speak. His breath is deep. He drops like a fallen sack down to the ground. I want to scream out to awaken him, but I cannot open my mouth. It is jammed shut. My thoughts swirl away like currents and I cannot bring them back.

Perhaps if I run, I think. But no, I will not leave my brother.

Something pulls me down. Down and down. There is no place to run to. No one to help us.

Just a few words come. I cling to them.

Hold fast!

Heaviness creeps up my legs and arms, then into my back. I feel myself tumbling down in a heap. Numbness. Sleep's spell crawls over me.

I fall into the dark underworld, dreaming.

CHAPTER 28

Place of Beginnings

NANA

Something pounds beneath me, shakes my head as it lies heavily upon the ground. It bounces along the riverbank and echoes in my ears. The sky is touched with pinks and reds. Sunset. Nanolatch nudges me awake. He points downstream, past the rapids, but keeps one finger on his lips. He crouches stiffly by the bank, lifting his head like a snake, sniffing a new scent on the air.

Downstream.

I feel it run right through me. Marking time. Beating hard.

Drumbeats on the wind. Louder by the minute.

I stand up. The cedar cape falls from my shoulders.

At my feet, the river runs faster than a thought. It is icy cold and so deep with spring rain that I cannot see the bottom.

"I hear the tribe coming. We lost time. The Ekas set a dreamspell on us." My brother yanks me away from the river. "Let's run to the mountains and hide. Hurry!"

My feet hug the riverbank like tree roots. Up and down my body goosebumps ripple, turning my skin silvery. Then, in the cool air, my body flushes red.

I know what I came here to do. What I was born for.

Paddles slap the water. Drums quicken their pace. Nanolatch pulls me away from the river, trying to lead me away.

"I didn't come here to hide." I yank free. "I must return to the Salmon House. If I stay with the tribe, I will never be free. I will drift in fog and dreams all my life."

I edge toward the river. Smolts dash downstream at my feet.

Nanolatch steps like a tree between the river and me.

"Don't leave, Salmonwife!" his words thunder above the river's roar.

That word, my sacred name, shimmers in the air between us, calling the spirits.

"Your destiny is with the tribe, Nanolatch. You will soon be the chief and transform the coast. That is what you and Noh promised me. The Way was planned for us all, long before we were born."

Nanolatch stares at me with dark, round eyes. Everything is suddenly still. We do not even hear the drumbeats any longer.

"I am the one they call to sea," I cry out.

My brother stands a head taller than me. He spreads his arms wide, encircling me.

"Step back!" I warn him.

Downstream, the rapids rush. Sharp boulders jut out here and there like knives. Drumbeats quicken.

Voices travel to us on the wind.

"Faster!" screams Shilka. "We are almost there. We must stop them before it is too late."

A million voices are calling me, chanting the ancient songs of the salmon. Words I once sang to them, words I told no one. They swell in my ears so I hear nothing else. I lift my arms up to the sky to touch the spirits swirling there. I pull them down into my chest, until they fill me.

Nanolatch turns to listen to the tribal voices on the wind. In that moment—the moment of magic—I push past him and dive straight into the cold running river.

Gone.

CHAPTER 29

NANOLATCH

I saw her long black hair fan out in the water—black lines pointing in many directions. She swam downstream toward the rapids with her body silvering in the river, her arms beating the cool spring air. She did not lift her head to breathe.

I waited, my harpoon dangling from my hands.

She did not turn around to look at me, standing upon shore with my face long and dark. I waited for her to surface, somewhere distant from where she dove in, as she always did.

She swam smoothly through the water. When she neared the rapids where the rocks jutted, she leaped high. Crimson bodied, her side was battered and beaten by the rocks. Still, she leaped a golden instant, spinning in the red blood of the sunset.

She disappeared beneath the water just as the tribe rounded the bend, twelve canoes riding straight toward me.

I flung my harpoon high so they all looked up. Its bone point trapped a ray of the dying sun, reflecting its brightness. It dazzled the fishermen. They never saw her swim past.

Then I slammed First Uncle's harpoon straight down and sliced it through my hair.

She was gone.

MYSTERY OF THE SALMON TWIN

NOH

She is the Salmon Being the Kwakiutls had long awaited. The one to sacrifice. The one to dive beneath the spring river. To return.

It is the Way.

At first she startled the young smolts with her long legs and long black hair. Through the bubbles they could dimly see her. They wondered how she breathed down there with them and why she did not surface. They saw her skin redden and shrink—as flesh does in cold water. On her legs grew pearly scales. Her back flamed berry red with silver hues. Pieces of her

fell off and lay on the river bottom. She stared
at the young fish, a pouch over her eyes—a
watery pouch that protected her deep brown
eyes.

Salmonwife.

All at once they knew her. The current took
them all.

Downstream. Down and down, tumbling to
the sea. Over rock and mud. Around fallen
trees. Through dark and shady waters,
Salmonwife led. The smolts gasped at her tail.
Swiftly the current swept them down. They
spilled out of the river's mouth and tasted their
first gulp of sea and its stinging salt taste. Salt
ran white through their veins. They flipped
over and over until it filled their gills. They
threw back their muscled heads and drank
deeply.

This was their remembering.

The sea held them in its slippery arms. The
tide drew them out—past the red cliffs and the
village, past the smoke that spiraled up, past
where the whales dove. Farther than they had
ever been. Miles deep. To where no one could
fish them out before their time.

Down they dropped.

Down into the depths where men cannot
travel. With her weight, Salmonwife dropped
quickly, and the young smolts sifted down
behind her. They fell helplessly, as if they had

come to an edge and had no choice. At first, all was darkness—murky deep. They knew only the silky touch of salt and sea.

Then the light.

The light shone from below like the glow of a winter's fire, calling them home. Then they reached the twin totems—Salmon Beings— carved into giant cedar posts. The house, built from rough red cedar, sat upon the floor of the sea. Salmonwife and the smolts tumbled down and down until they fell in front of the door.

Light was reflected from a thousand Salmon Men inside. Silvery red fish, their scales glistening in the bright light of the Salmon House. All waited for her to come home.

Salmonwife entered. The young smolts followed.

She remembered.

CHAPTER 30

Nanolatch Remembering

NOH

He stands at the riverbank, the breeze she stirred touching his skin still. Layers of their past peel away and float on the water behind her.

Salmonwife.

She whose voice called the salmon. She who remembered the dark underworld from where they came.

Chiefs come and go. One dies and another takes his place. Salmon Men visit once from their house of eternal time and are never forgotten.

His tears fall, releasing the tightness of his heart and the wall between them. A wall he would not, could not, cross. His salt tears fall into the river to join the water rolling down to sea.

He must go back to the Place of Mists.

It will never be enough now, he thinks. His destiny. He swallows it like a hook snagging a fish's mouth. He wonders if somehow she hears the thoughts that fly from his soul.

He greets the tribe, drags their canoes onto the banks, shrugs his shoulders at their questions, and waits—as he will always watch and wait—for her. He looks downstream in Nana's trail. Homeward.

He cannot follow her.

His words and tears sift down between the rocks, spiral in pools, and bounce in deep waters until they reach the Salmon House by the sea. They spill inside—words of the heart, spoken over water, waiting to be heard.

Nanolatch, know this, wherever you are. Your sister opens wide her mouth and swallows your tears that fell down and down into the sea.

Place of Mists

CHAPTER 31

U'mista

Three Years Later

NANOLATCH

Every fall the geese make a great squawking, darkening the sky with their yearning to go back home. I watch them disappear, wishing I could fly among them, instead of dropping cedar lines for halibut.

Southward.

If Noh lives, if she reached her village safely, she will be chanting by the shoreline as these same geese pass overhead. She will look up at them, as I do, and stop. Maybe she will smile at how they always travel back and forth between the two of us. She will listen, as only shamans can, for the messages they bear. For surely these birds have seen me here by the shore, looking toward the Salmon

House and crying out.

I wonder if Noh thinks of me, or knows what has become of us. News travels on the tribal coast. She may have heard the story—how one, a Kwakiutl girl, guessed the mystery only the ancients knew. The secret of transforming one flesh into another. Human into animal. Girl into Salmonwife.

My hair touches my shoulder blades again. I would cut it all over again if I could bring one of them back. I am the ghost that travels between the two girls—the shell they left behind. When the day's work is done, I have no one to turn to, no friend who I love. No girl here strong enough in spirit to call me to her as they did. These village girls are flesh and blood, not of the spirit. None have eyes to see into me. When I looked at my sister, I saw myself and what she believed of me.

All that I am. All that I will become. All waiting.

These three years have passed with the days all melting into one another. Lean years. We do not journey to the river where the fish no longer run. The Kwakiutls hunt instead, eating the flesh of animals and bitter herbs from the woods. We gather clams and scallops, dig mussels, and fish for cod and halibut all year long—even summer—by the sea. No rest. No baskets are brimful with salmon. No potlatch brightens the empty Ceremonial House. No dark winter nights are spent huddled by the fire, storytelling in the smoky air.

One spring day, after we haul in our catch, I stop
on the beach to watch the geese return to us. I study
each one. Which one has Noh looked at as they
were flying away? Perhaps their leader—the one
with the longest blue-green tail. We may each have
touched the same ones with our eyes. At least I have
that much of her.

The wind lifts from the south. The first spring
wind. From somewhere far off, I hear pounding.

Drumbeats tiny as a pulse. Two beats.

Then nothing.

Then two beats again.

I look out to sea. Beyond the bay, past the whitecaps, something is stirring. A brightness. Light pulses
from the Salmon House. Once before, I saw it glimmer like that, when my sister ended her fasting trial.
But it has been dim these three years.

"Do you see it out there?" I call to a fisherman
walking past.

He turns to where I point. "See what?"

I run to find Second Uncle in the plankhouse. I
yank him out to shore.

"Do you notice anything out there?" I ask him.
He scans the horizon with narrowed eyes.

"What do you see, Nanolatch?"

I don't know if I should tell him. Soon Father
and Shilka pass by. They stand there as if nothing
has changed, speaking only about the weather turning to spring.

"Nanolatch thinks he sees something," teases

Second Uncle. "A whale perhaps. Or a sea monster."
All three of them look out together and laugh.
They do not see what I do, shining there, glowing
brighter by the minute. Beating out such a chant, it
makes me lift up my feet.

Nana lives! I thought her gone forever. I spin
upon the shoreline, with my hands upside down on
the beach, stirring up so much sand it whips in
everyone's faces. The fishermen shake their heads at
me. Even Father smiles, for I have been silent these
past years.

"You will be glad to hear this, son," he tells me.
"Shilka says it is time to return upriver. But first we
must talk."

What can this mean that it shines like that?
And now we are called back to the sacred grounds?
Somewhere my sister is stirring! Soon I might see
her again.

Shilka must sense it too, but he does not see the
light. He sniffs it on the wind. I feel something lift
me up as if my feet no longer stand upon the
ground. I soar straight up. My heart is as high as
those journeying geese.

My father draws me away from the fishermen.
We stop beneath the totem poles.

"If...when the salmon return, there will be
enough food for everyone on the coast," he says.
"Time for potlatches. Long winters of rest. Peace."

It takes me a while to speak. My pulse rushes—
loud and wild, like a river.

"Does everyone believe this will happen?"

"We long for it, son. We will rejoice when the salmon return. Then you will be chief."

I gasp. "How can this happen? You are alive and well! Why should I rule the tribe?"

"I cannot say when this time will be. Now or many years distant. But it will come. You will just know it. A moment will come when your judgement will be better than mine. Act. You will bring us a great future."

"What will my duties be as chief?"

"To catch the First Salmon. Greet neighboring tribes. Reign over potlatch. And to wed. I hope to find you a wife soon. None I have seen so far are noble enough."

When my father first saw my mother at the Nootka potlatch to honor his chiefhood, he decided upon her. But there is no girl here who I would want as wife.

The one I want was a slave once.

Later that spring, when the salmonberries ripen juicy sweet, I lead the tribe upriver. It is the first honor of my manhood, delayed these three long years. I stand in the bow of the head canoe, my eyes searching the water like beams of sunshine. Shifting. Watching. Waiting. No fish to be seen.

When we reach our spot, all is darkness. Yet around us is movement. A rustle of evergreen branches. A sweep of wind. The rush of clear water over rock.

A whispering of spirit voices from the mountain-top.

I lie that night like a stone upon the cold earth, sinking down into a deep sleep. When I awake, spirit voices buzz all around me, singing louder and louder. Voices my sister alone must have heard. Although she stood right beside me before her leap, she was already far away, in another country.

The air hums. The wind blows the voices down the mountain and sweeps them into the river. Feet pound the ground. I race to the river behind the fishermen.

Fifty men strong wait by the river. We listen to a great thrashing from downstream, a beating upon the water. A silvery run of Chinook salmon. Hundreds of fish swarm upstream shoulder to shoulder. We can hear them splashing as they turn into the river from the sea. Just like the fishing tales of First Uncle. Father runs off for his spear. But the rest of us stand still.

I wait.

One by one, salmon leap over the waterfall. Silvery fish swim to the leader who points out the way they must travel. The lead salmon edges back to the rim of the pool, beats with a slap of its fins upon the water, beats with a pound of its tail like the boom of drums. It leaps twenty feet high in the air. Higher than I have seen any fish jump.

Father crouches low. He is ready for the

moment. The magic moment. He poses his weapon in midair and shoots it.

In that moment, my hand stretches out and grabs the spear as it flies by. My arm vibrates like a tight bowstring.

All eyes turn to watch the salmon. It twirls above us, round-bellied, a long streak flowing down its back like long black hair. It shouts a great cry that echoes over the water like a warrior's voice. It spins and looks at me a moment before scaling the waterfall.

A silver moment.

Gone.

The fishermen fall on their knees, surrounding me.

I hear Father's voice calling. "Well done, Chief! The salmon have returned to honor you."

The rest of the school leaps above the waterfall, one by one. I crouch low. Then I lift the spear and shoot it. It lands clear through the back of the last fish in the pool. The men stir, splashing into the waters, fifty men strong, shouting and lifting a Chinook salmon above their heads to touch the sun.

Warriors' cries echo across the mountains all that day. The salmon, long gone, are at last reborn.

*

On the last day of midsummer when we leave upriver, the fishwives gather strips of salmon from the drying racks. They fill a hundred baskets on the ground. Though the fish are plentiful, I ordered that we capture only one in twenty. Sacrifice. Never again would we wish to be without the salmon.

As I swim beneath the waterfall, I smile to think how I am free to go to her now. Weave back the life we once stole from her and all her village. Build the longhouses we burned down. Bring the light back to Noh. Atonement—something given for what was lost. That is U'mista.

My tribe believes that this waiting, without fishing in the sacred grounds, was our atonement. But they are wrong. For me, it was living without her.

Even Father says that, when he returns home, he will travel once again to the Country Beyond the Ocean. Drop his prayers down into the water and ask for forgiveness.

"She was the one they called," he confesses. "I thought I could protect Nana. Marry her to the Nootkas. But I couldn't stop the Way. I never should have tried. She has saved us all instead."

Some wait for death to say such prayers. But I won't. As soon as I return to the coast, I will set out for Salish land. Living shall be my prayer.

Just as I splash out, something nibbles at my fingers and toes underwater. I look upstream at the crystal clear waterfall. Leaping down from the waterfall are a thousand baby salmon. A thousand salmon running where once there was one.

Author's Note

This novel began when I heard a Kwakiutl transformation myth. In the pre-contact era (before the European explorers) when the salmon runs were sometimes meager, this tribe believed that male warriors could dive into water to become salmon. The sacrifice was thought to regenerate the natural world. This myth would become my ending, although I didn't know it at the time. All I knew is that I was haunted by the image of that diving warrior. It sunk deeply into my mind and heart.

As I visited the Northwest over the years, I sensed how such a supernatural belief could be born. I was drawn in, like fog, by the landscape. Cedar trees poking up like poles. The rocky shoreline. Ravens croaking overhead. Mists that swallow distant mountains. The wild sea. The tribes who lived on this coast saw it as a reflection of a larger spiritual world.

Kwakiutl is a name commonly used for a whole group, but it actually refers to one tribe in Fort Rupert. The term "Kwakwaka'wakw" is now used for all those who speak the same language—Kwakwala—in British Columbia. Its twelve pre-contact tribes hunted and gathered food during the warm months, followed by winters of spiritual rituals. They were considered the wealthiest of all Native Americans due to the abundance of their natural environment—mild weather and a surplus of wildlife in the sea and on the land. Their art, storytelling, and myths flourished. Their chief, a descendant of an animal ancestor, was responsible for keeping the balance of nature and ensuring that the animals upon which the tribe depended would reappear each successive year. At the potlatch, wealth was shared and exchanged within a tribal system, a way of ensuring that nature would always flourish.

Understanding the ancient Kwakiutls is a complex task. We are far removed in time from pre-contact society, which had an oral tradition. When the anthropologist Franz Boas arrived in the late nineteenth century to do research, native customs had almost disappeared. William Elmendorf, Irving Goldman, Claude Levi-Strauss and Helen Codere further developed theories in the twentieth century. Modern viewpoints, however, like those of Leland Donald and Joseph Masco, have challenged previous conceptions of issues like slavery and class systems among the early northwest tribes. It is evident that the history of the pre-contact world is currently still being written.

This is a work of fiction set in an imaginary Kwakiutl village far north of present-day Vancouver, B.C. Since I found much controversy and contradiction in my research, along with a revision of earlier interpretations, my approach was to write a fictional account of Kwakiutl history accessible to today's reader. While I tried to provide authenticity in depicting the pre-contact life of the Kwakiutl, I still had to remain true to my characters, who had created their own world and understood it through their viewpoints. Certain aspects, like their names, tattooing, the Salmon Being chant, and beliefs concerning the creature Sisiutl, are my own interpretations. The ceremonies and rituals in the transformation potlatch have been altered and simplified to suit this story. Any mistakes in historical fact are mine.

Throughout my research, I absorbed what remains of the past—the art of the northwest coast people, which transmits a powerful sense of native beliefs. The towering totem poles at the Museum of Anthropology at the University of British Columbia, and the Royal British Columbia Provincial Museum in Victoria. The masks in the Museum at Campbell River. Bill Reid's drawing of a Killer Whale Spirit. A transformation mask exhibit in Thunder Bay. Photographs of Edward Curtis taken when native culture was dwindling. The initiation dress of a Kwakiutl girl at the American Museum of Natural History in New York City.

This book was made possible with the assistance of many: Ann Featherstone, my incredible editor, who loves the Northwest and First Nations lore; Judge Scow, a Kwakwaka'wakw elder, for his insightful review of the manuscript; The Society of Children's Book Writers and Illustrators, who awarded the draft a Works-in-Progress grant; the U'mista Cultural Society, Alert Bay; Maxine Bruce, Aboriginal Fisheries Coordinator, Port Hardy, for her wonderful fishing information; Divina Hunt, Kwakiutl Treaty Coordinator, Port Hardy, for her discussions; William Fry, fish development, University of California; and Frieda Gates, my mentor from Empire State College.

The First Nations people believe that the salmon are messengers who predict our future. What happens to them affects us all. The salmon, which have migrated up rivers for thousands of years, are rapidly disappearing. Commercial logging, the building of dams, industrial pollution, urbanization, and commercial overfishing have together endangered the migrating salmon. To me, this transformation myth is a plea for a return to balance and conservation before it is too late. We must all find ways to perform U'mista—to give back what belongs to this earth so that it will remain with us always in our oceans, wildlife, the forests, and the air.

GLOSSARY

Bella Coola (Bell-a cool-a), or Nuxalk: a tribe living on the north side of the Bella Coola River in British Columbia

Big House: permanent cedar plank dwellings by the sea that housed extended families; also referred to as plankhouse, or longhouse (Salish)

Chinook salmon (shi-nook): the first salmon to run in the spring, one of which can weigh up to 120 pounds (45 kilograms)

Dzonokwa (Zu-ne-kwa): a supernatural being; a wild woman living deep in the woods; kidnapper of children; one who assists young girls in the trials of Initiation

Ekas (eek-cas): evil spirits

eulachon (OO-lak-en), or oolachon, or eulachan: a type of migrating herring, also called candlefish; useful for light and cooking oil

Haida (Hy-dah): a tribe on the west coast of the Queen Charlotte Islands and southern Prince of Wales Island in British Columbia

Kwakiutl (Kwa-kee-oo-tul): the name of one tribe located at Fort. Rupert; also a common name for Kwakwaka'wakw, or Nak'waxdaxw, who are Kwakwala-speaking people living on the northwest coast of British Columbia and Vancouver Island

Lequiltok (Lee-quill-talk): a Kwakwaka'wakw tribe from the southernmost part of Kwakiutl territory on Vancouver Island

michimis (mish-ee-mi): commoner(s)

Nootka (Newt-ka): a tribe living on the west coast of Vancouver Island; also called Nuu-chah-nulth

potlatch (pot-lach): a ceremony that includes a feast,
dancing, storytelling, and gift giving—to celebrate a
marriage, death, birth or Initiation

Salish (Saa-lish): a large northwest tribe living around the
Vancouver Island/Vancouver/Seattle area, along the
northwest coast, and in the interior region of British
Columbia

Sisiutl (Sis-u-tl): a double-headed serpent, a
Kwakwaka'wakw mythological creature of the sea

sockeye salmon: the slimmest salmon with the reddish
flesh when cooked

taise (taas): royalty, of the chief's family

Tsetseka (Te-sak-a), also Tsitsika: the sacred time during
winter when the spirits are closer to the earth

U'mista (u-mist-a): the return of that which was taken,
originating in early times when captives taken in
raids were returned to their homes.